'You're a be[...]
had realised[...]
diagnosis was[...]
improved.'

'Good. But still a bit—fragile?'

'Nurses can't afford fragile. We have work to do.'

'I know. And you know that you and this unit are doing an excellent job. Remember I told you when we first met about an incubator that somehow got cold? Risking the baby's life? I know that wouldn't happen now, and that's because of you. We lost Baby Hellaby. No unit in the country could have done more for him. You should think of our cases that are successful—not the opposite.'

'It's because it all is so random,' she said. 'It makes you think that nothing is worth chancing.'

'In this life you have to take chances,' he said. 'Otherwise you get nothing.'

SPECIAL CARE BABY UNIT

**Special babies, special carers—
lives lived moment to moment . . .
heartbeat to heartbeat**

Dear Reader

My daughter Helen trained as a midwife, but now works mostly in a SCBU. I have seen her feeding a baby so small that she could hold it in one hand. It's work that she loves. It's hard, but so often rewarding.

SCBU work is intensive. The staff—doctors, nurses, ancillary workers—are thrown together in an intimate and often intense working environment. This intimacy often affects their personal lives. It is that very intimacy, and the level of care that I saw being administered to those tiny babies, that influenced me to write this series of stories.

The Consultant's Rescue is the first novel in my new trilogy set in a SCBU in the Wolds Hospital in Denham.

There are two more stories to follow, each featuring a dedicated heroine who discovers that you need more than work to be completely fulfilled.

I hope that you enjoy reading them.

With best wishes,

Gill Sanderson

**Read the next book in this heartrending series
coming soon from Mills & Boon®
Medical Romance™**

THE CONSULTANT'S RESCUE

BY

GILL SANDERSON

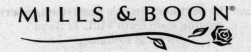

MILLS & BOON®

For Big Ed, the heart of the Rugby Club

First published in Great Britain 2004
Harlequin Mills & Boon Limited,
Eton House, 18-24 Paradise Road, Richmond, Surrey TW9 1SR

© Gill Sanderson 2004

ISBN 0 263 83888 9

Set in Times Roman 10½ on 12¼ pt.
03-0304-48141

Printed and bound in Spain
by Litografia Rosés, S.A., Barcelona

CHAPTER ONE

IT WAS no hardship for Jane Wilson to be up early. She had not slept really well since…well, since. So, though her motel bed was comfortable, she had risen, thrown on the nearest clothes and walked to her car. Now she was standing on the beach, staring at the everlasting waves.

This was different from London. She could see the sun, rising from the east over the sea. To her right the beach swept on, apparently endlessly. To her left were high white cliffs. There was the sound of gulls crying, the rhythmic beat of the sea on the sand. And everywhere the pervasive smell of salt. She liked it here.

In the distance, coming from the little town, she saw a jogger. In no time he was passing her, shouting a cheerful, 'Gorgeous day, isn't it?'

'Absolutely gorgeous,' she shouted back, and watched him till he was just a coloured spot on the sand. Once she'd run to keep fit. Perhaps she could start again.

Suddenly she realised just how much she'd wanted to move here. She could start a new life, perhaps after a while even be happy again. Of course it would be a fight. The jump in rank from Sister to Ward Manager was a big one. But perhaps a fight was what she needed. It was what he would have wanted. The thought of him gave her new strength. She *would* start a new life. If not here, why, then, somewhere else. As she so often did, almost unconsciously, she twisted her wedding ring, took it off and kissed it. Then she slid it back on.

She glanced at her watch. Time was passing, she needed to be just a little bit early. And calm and in control.

Back in her motel room she showered, quickly dried her short blonde hair. For the interview she had bought a new dress. It seemed so long since she had bought any new clothes. But this was a sober, efficient dress. Smart, not dowdy, well cut and in an obviously expensive fabric. But it suggested a person who was in control. It was blue and now she realised it looked rather like a nurse's uniform.

She looked at herself in the full-length mirror, a detached, appraising look. No unsightly bumps or creases. The dress didn't hide her femininity, her arms were still good, her breasts generous, John would have said... The pain of memory lanced through her like a scalpel cutting flesh. For the moment forget him! Not that she could. But she had to be strong.

She forced her hand to stop trembling, put on her normal restrained make-up. Then looked again. Yes, she would do. She might not get the job, but she'd put up a good fight.

Outside it was getting even warmer. Unlike London, there was no smell of traffic fumes, but still the everpresent smell of the sea. She liked this little bit of the Yorkshire coast.

For a moment she couldn't see her car—surely no one would have stolen the rusty old thing? But then she remembered she was not looking for her large station wagon. That she had got rid of quickly, it had too many memories. Instead she had bought a tiny red car, exactly big enough for her and her alone.

She liked the look of the Wolds Hospital. It was on a small hill just on the outskirts of the little seaside town of Denham. You could easily walk into town from it. She drove through tree-shaded lawns, looking at the older red-brick buildings and the new constructions. A big building programme here. Plenty of parking space, too. Jane liked what she had seen so far.

She followed the map she had been sent, went into Reception and was directed to a waiting room where she was greeted by a smiling middle-aged secretary. 'Jane Wilson? I'm Marjory Edwards, secretary to the chief administrative officer. Do sit down. Would you like a coffee or perhaps a drink of water or juice?'

'Water would be fine,' Jane said. She didn't want her caffeine levels too high.

Marjory ticked off her name on a list, then fetched the water—with ice and a slice of lemon, Jane noted. Then she lifted her phone and said, 'Mrs Wilson is here, Mr Carrington—yes, about five minutes.'

Replacing the receiver, she said, 'We have five candidates for the position, Mrs Wilson. The board will see them at hourly intervals. We hope to give you a decision at about five o'clock. Now, could you just fill in this expenses form for me, please?'

Jane dipped into her bag for the bills she had brought ready. As well to be prepared.

It really was quite nice here, she thought. She could be happy here. It was a while since she had been interviewed for a job, but surprisingly she felt quite calm. This wasn't good! If she wanted the job then she should try to fight for it. Get away from the feeling that nothing really mattered.

The phone rang and after a muttered conversation Marjory went through double mahogany doors and then came out and said, 'The board would like to see you now, Mrs Wilson.'

Jane stood, took a deep breath. Now for the fight.

Marjory took her into the room, pulled out a chair so she could sit at one end of a brightly polished table. Jane made herself comfortable, took a second to glance round the room. This was in the old part of the hospital, with panelled walls and oil paintings of long-forgotten dignitaries. There was also a side table with a computer terminal on it. The Wolds Hospital was up to date.

At the top of the table five people were sitting. An older, pleasant man stood and smiled. He said, 'Hello, Mrs Wilson, I am Paul Carrington, Chief Administrative Officer of the Wolds Hospital. On my left we have Mary White, the senior nurse here, and Peter Knowles, our finance officer. On my right is Ms Fay Donahue who is in charge of Human Resources. And, finally, Mr Fielding, who is one of the two consultants in the neonatal unit.'

As they were introduced, most of the board members smiled and mumbled a greeting. Jane thought she detected a touch of fellow feeling in the smile of Fay Donahue. Perhaps she'd been through this recently herself. The last person to be introduced, Chris Fielding, didn't speak. He inclined his head, smiled briefly, as if his thoughts were elsewhere. He looked to be a striking but a thoughtful man and Jane guessed that his questions might be troublesome. Well, she would cope.

'Before we start, I'd like to make something clear,' Paul Carrington said. 'The trust has decided to develop and expand the Wolds Hospital here at Denham. It is in process of closing down the Princess Mary Hospital twelve miles away in Calthorpe. We believe that this amalgamation will eventually be in the best interests of staff and patients.'

He sipped from his glass of water. 'In particular, the neonatal unit in Calthorpe has been closed down and the staff transferred here. There has been a lot of bad feeling among the staff, a lot of uncertainty. The leaders of both units—here and at Calthorpe—have both left. One has retired, one has gone to a senior job in Birmingham. We need someone who can pull the new unit together and so we advertised for a new ward manager. Now...' he smiled again '...I'd like you to start by telling us about yourself and your nursing experience and qualifications.'

She had expected this question, had thought about it and researched it. How to get all the important facts across without going on too long. So she spoke and at the end of five minutes Paul Carrington nodded approvingly. 'Very satisfactory,' he said. 'Now, I've told you about our amalgamation. How would you deal with a member of your staff who has been transferred and is now complaining bitterly about her new conditions?'

A tricky one. Jane thought for a minute and then said, 'I'd first see if there was any genuine cause for her complaint. If there was, I'd try to put it right. But in general I would say that the new unit is providing a better service to the public. Our neonates now stand a better chance. Nurses are professionals. We do not take our ill feelings out on our patients.'

'Isn't that a bit harsh?'

'No. Staff are happier if they know where they stand.' Jane hesitated and then said, 'But I would feel very guilty if I didn't know that we were providing a better service.'

'Quite so. Now, you say in your application form that…'

It was a gruelling interview. The panel knew what they wanted and the questions they asked were searching. But Jane kept calm, thought for a couple of moments if she was not quite sure of her answer and at times admitted that there was something that she just didn't know.

Finally it was the turn of Chris Fielding to question her. Something told her that this man would be the hardest to convince. He looked thoughtful, assessing. He would be the man she would be working with—or working for. This was the man who had most to gain or lose by this appointment.

He didn't speak at first, just looked at her. But she managed to look back at him coolly, confidently.

'This is a new unit. We need someone to devote all their time and energies over the next two or three years to get it running smoothly. There must be no breaks. Are you capable of that devotion?' He paused a moment, gave her that brief smile she had seen before and then went on, 'And, please, don't just say, "Yes, of course I am."'

He was challenging her. She looked at him again, more closely this time. So far he had only been a man in a dark suit. Now she saw the muscular shoulders, the trim body and the slightly long dark hair. She guessed he was in his early thirties, young for a consultant. His expression, his eyes, were calm, distant. She couldn't tell what colour his eyes were. When he smiled, he was quite attractive. But he didn't smile too often. What was on his mind?

The question was obviously designed to test her. She knew what he was getting at and she decided to fight back. 'It sounds as if you are asking me, as a married woman, if I'm likely to have children in the next few years,' she said. 'As I'm sure you know, such a question would be most improper. But I'll answer it. I am a widow. I have no children. I have no intention of remarrying and certainly no intention of having children. Yes, I am capable of the devotion you require.'

Paul Carrington spoke then, very quickly. 'I am sure that Mr Fielding didn't intend to ask a question which, as you say, would be most improper. But thank you for your honest answer. Chris, have you any more questions?'

'No. I am satisfied.' He smiled at Jane. 'I'm sorry if you felt I was being personal and I apologise. I was only trying to do my best for the unit.'

He doesn't look very sorry, Jane thought, and gave him a cold little smile back.

'Then I think your ordeal is over, Mrs Wilson,' Paul said, smiling and reassuring. 'Now, we hope to have a decision by five this afternoon. No need for you to hang around. Why not have a walk in the sun?'

As if by magic, Marjory appeared at Jane's elbow and escorted her out of the room. Jane felt battered. It had been a hard three quarters of an hour.

'Have a sit-down for a few minutes,' Marjory said, leading Jane back to a chair in her office. 'I'll fetch you a coffee now. I'll bet you need it.'

'Yes, I'd like a coffee.' Jane leaned back, closed her eyes, sighed and tried to relax her shoulders. She had been more tense than she'd realised.

Then she opened her eyes and realised that there was someone sitting opposite her.

The woman smiled, stretched a hand across the coffee-table. 'Hi. I'm Fiona Law—we're after the same job. May the best woman win and all that sort of thing.'

'Hi. I'm Jane Wilson. As you say, may the best woman win.'

She looked at the woman curiously as so far she had not met any of the other candidates. Fiona Law looked confident. She was a bit older than herself—say in her early thirties. Her dark suit was obviously expensive but Jane thought that the skirt was just a touch too short for a formal meeting. Her make-up had obviously taken quite a long time and her long blonde hair curled down her back.

'Where are you from?' Fiona asked, pleasantly enough. 'I know you're not local, I know all the local candidates.'

'I'm from London.' Jane named her own prestigious hospital. 'Are you from around here?'

'Born and bred. I suppose I'm the sitting candidate.' Fiona gave a self-satisfied laugh. 'I've been here ages—in fact, I did most of the work of running the unit. Poor old Marcia Kent, who has retired, just couldn't cope.'

'I see,' said Jane.

'But don't worry, I'm sure the interview will be fair,' Fiona went on. 'You'll be given your chance.'

'I'm not worrying.' Jane wasn't worrying. But she was getting increasingly irritated.

Marjory came over. 'Miss Law, the committee will see you now.' With a blinding smile Fiona stood, smoothed her short skirt and swayed towards the committee room. Jane decided it would be too hypocritical to wish her good luck and so stayed silent.

'Would you like another coffee?' Marjory asked. 'You must have had quite a hard time.' There was sympathy in her smile and Jane guessed that the secretary was referring to listening to Fiona rather than the interview. Fiona was obviously not everyone's best friend.

'Not too hard a time, nothing I can't cope with,' she said cheerfully, 'but, yes, I'd love another coffee. And then I think I'll go for a walk.'

'A very good idea,' said Marjory. 'You don't want to spend all your time chatting.'

For a moment she stood, just looking round and enjoying the grass, the trees, the difference in the air. There were little green and white signposts everywhere and she looked for one that might direct her to the SCBU, the special care baby unit where she hoped to work. She wondered what it was like.

'Are you lost?'

A voice behind her, deep and calm. She turned to see Chris Fielding. He looked even more imposing standing up but he seemed quite friendly and she felt happier.

'I thought I might look at the outside of the unit,'

she said. 'You know we were told that it would not be possible to look round before the interview.'

'I'm afraid that was my decision. We're short-staffed and I want to keep disturbance to a minimum. But if you come with me now I'm sure we can give you a glimpse for a few minutes.' He strode on in silence for a moment and then said, 'I'm concerned about one of my charges. She's twenty-nine forty, we just can't get her to gain weight. I suspect some kind of bug is making her vomit—but we can't identify it.'

'I see.' Jane recognised the shorthand. A baby born prematurely, at twenty-nine weeks instead of the usual forty. For them, early life was a struggle, there was only a fifty-fifty chance of survival.

'So using a nasogastric tube wouldn't be a good idea. Are you feeding her intravenously?' she asked.

'No, I decided to go beyond the stomach. I've inserted a transpyloric tube, feeding milk straight into the small intestine.' He looked at her thoughtfully. 'A technique you're familiar with?'

'Of course. We had a case, a baby I nursed two months ago. Successfully, I might add.'

'I'm pleased to hear that. This particular child suffered because her incubator temperature wasn't checked. It was no one's fault, I looked into it, just a consequence of too few nurses. But now that baby is just hanging onto life. I'm hoping that the new appointee will stop that kind of thing.'

Jane winced. Neonates needed a precisely calculated temperature if they were to survive. Too hot and they lost energy by sweating; too cold and they lost energy by shivering. And they didn't have much energy to spare.

There was another pause in the conversation and then she said, 'You'd be my consultant if I got this job?'

'I would. There is another paediatric consultant but I'm the one who specialises in the neonatal side. Do you think you could work with me?'

'I can work with anyone if they are professional,' she said coolly.

'Good. Then we will—sorry, we would—get on. I approve of being professional.' They paced on a little further and then he said, 'In the interview, you suggested that my question to you was unprofessional.'

'I did. And you know I was right.'

He chuckled, and it made him seem more human. 'You were right, it was unprofessional. But I thought you were a good candidate and a good candidate deserves a hard question.'

'One way of looking at things,' she said. It struck her that there was more to Mr Fielding than she had at first thought

Yet another pause. He evidently didn't see the need to indulge in unnecessary chit-chat. Then something struck her. 'You're not interviewing?' she asked.

'No, I withdrew for this one session. I can't interview fairly because the candidate is my sister-in-law. It could be said that there is a conflict of interests. I shan't vote either. But I'll attend the interviews of the other candidates and I shall help with the deliberations at the end. I believe this to be a very important appointment.'

They had reached a new building, an attractive single-storey wing to the main hospital. He led her through the waiting room, nodding briskly at the receptionist, and turned to the neonatal ward. There he tapped in the code that opened the door. Jane sighed. She knew it was necessary, but to have to lock a ward in case of crime seemed to her to be so sad.

Inside she felt instantly at home. There was that atmosphere, that smell that was subtly different from all other wards. She loved it, this was where she worked.

'If you would wait here a minute, Mrs Wilson?' Chris Fielding pushed through a door. A moment later he returned with a smiling woman in green scrubs. 'This is Sister Erica Thornby,' the consultant said. 'Erica, if you have time, could you show Mrs Wilson here a little of the unit? If you're too busy, send her back to Reception.' He looked at Jane. 'Is that all right?'

'I wouldn't have it any other way.'

Sister Erica Thornby, another member of the staff of the unit. Jane looked at her and thought that she would like her better than Fiona Law. Erica was a pretty woman in her mid-thirties, her dark hair in a French pleat.

'I'm just going to do the obs on a couple of the babies,' Fiona said. 'D'you want to borrow a gown and a mask? Then we can talk as I work.'

'Love to,' said Jane. 'Where can I scrub up?' No way was she walking into a ward without being as infection-free as it was possible to get.

'Follow me,' said Erica.

There were three babies in the little ward, all in incubators. Jane recognised that these weren't high-risk babies. She could tell by their movements that they were gaining in strength. At the moment there were no parents there, this meant they could talk. Jane watched as Erica deftly recorded temperature, blood pressure and breathing rate.

'Where are you from?' Erica asked, when things were running smoothly. 'Why do you especially want to come here?'

It seemed that everyone was asking the same question. So she gave the same, honest answer—even if it was only half of one. 'I'm from London. I need a change, a complete change. And this looks a well set-up unit.'

There was silence for a moment and then Erica said carefully, 'This is just my opinion. But we need a leader. Trying to amalgamate two departments has been a nightmare. Some of us need a good kicking. There have been too many meetings, too much trying to suit everyone. Holidays, shift times, two people thinking they're entitled to the same single job, we argue over everything. Somehow they've taken two happy departments and turned them into one miserable one. Which is daft, because most of us really love the work.'

'I see,' said Jane. 'I was talking to one of your colleagues—Fiona Law. She must stand a good chance of getting the job.'

Erica's face was turned away from Jane, but in the reflection from the glass in the door she saw the sister grimace. 'Possibly,' she said.

'Apparently the sister-in-law of the consultant?'

'True. But that won't sway Chris Fielding. He does everything perfectly properly, he's a stickler for the rules.'

'But you like him?'

'I do. He's super with the kids, he's very thoughtful

of the parents, he'll help anyone so long as they're willing to work. Of course, it takes a while to get to know him. Don't be fooled by that abstracted air he has. He knows exactly what he's doing.'

'I can imagine,' Jane said.

Erica lifted the lid of an incubator and lifted out the baby. Cradling the tiny thing in one hand, she reached for the ready prepared bottle and eased it to the pink mouth. The baby started sucking at once, and Erica smiled down. 'You're learning, little Harry,' she murmured. 'This is your mum's milk, and it's so, so good for you.'

Jane looked on approvingly. She could work with Erica.

After a while Erica asked, 'If you come here, if you get the job…have you…? I see you're wearing a wedding ring.'

'I was married, now I am a widow. And I have no children.'

'Oh, I'm sorry. I—'

'It doesn't matter, Erica, it's over now.' Jane decided to change the subject. 'Are you married?'

'Not yet. I've lived with the same man for five years, perhaps we ought to… I'd like a family and I'm getting on a bit…' Erica laughed, but Jane realised she had accidentally touched a raw nerve. The other woman had been just a little too falsely bright. And it was just a bit early to be exchanging intimate details.

At that moment one of the other babies woke and started to cry. Strange how they knew when was the most inconvenient time. Erica walked over and peered down. 'You'll have to wait, baby McKay,' she said. 'Got my hands full at the moment.'

But baby McKay paid no attention. He carried on screaming, his naked little body jerking on the mattress.

Jane listened for a moment and then said. 'If it's only feeding, would you like me to…?'

'Thanks,' Erica said promptly. 'The feed's over there, you know what to do.'

Indeed, Jane did know what to do. She picked up the baby, felt that instant stab of love and compassion for someone so small. The little body stopped squirming, the blue eyes stared at her, unfocussed. Jane reached for the bottle. Baby McKay was hungry.

For a while she forgot she was at the hospital to be interviewed, she was doing what she knew and liked. Erica had recognised her competence at once and had not hesitated to leave the room to mark up the obs. And when Jane finally stopped to place the now dozing baby back in his incubator, she discovered that Chris Fielding had stepped silently into the ward.

He looked at her thoughtfully. 'I can see you're very competent, Mrs Wilson,' he said. 'But as yet you are not a member of staff of this hospital. I don't even know if you're insured. I'm not sure that I'm happy with what you're doing.'

She said nothing until she had settled the baby in his incubator. Then she stepped back, pointed and said, 'He approves. He's happy. There's no way I'm going to stand back and let a baby suffer when I think I can stop it.'

She saw him think about this. Then he said, 'Of course, you're quite right. But now I think that it's time that we left.'

'You've seen your patient?'

For the first time he smiled fully and his face was transformed. 'I have. She needs no help from us, she's recovering on her own. She's putting on weight and looking much happier. Let's just say that I'm now looking forward to seeing her father this evening, instead of dreading it.'

He led her outside, told her to remember to be back for the interview decision at five o'clock, said good morning and strode off briskly. This was turning into a full day, she thought as she watched him disappear.

She glanced at her watch. She had hours yet, so she set off to walk down into the little town. Would she like working with Chris Fielding? She thought she rather would. He was competent, reasonably friendly, but much of the time his thoughts were obviously elsewhere. Just what she wanted. Of course, he was attractive—when he smiled, really attractive—but he was probably married to Fiona Law's sister. Jane wondered what his wife was like, how it would be to be married to such a man. Not her business. Anyway, she hadn't got the job yet.

She liked Denham, it was so different from London. It was both a seaside town and a centre for the local farming community. There were a lot of holidaymakers but not as many as there would have been before Continental holidays had become so popular. Many of the people she saw were probably locals. She passed through what she heard called the Old Town, very different from the seaside frontage. She'd like to live here.

At lunchtime she found a café by the harbour, an

ordinary place with plastic tables and pictures of trawlers on the walls. She just had to order fish and chips. The meal was fantastic and it cost her about half what it would have cost in London. When she said this to the smiling waitress she was told that the fish had been in the sea that morning and the chips were from potatoes from a farm not ten miles away.

She walked out, looked down at the harbour and then—as happened so often—memories tore apart the life she was trying to build herself. It was so clear, like yesterday! Eating fish and chips with John at a little café near the hospital. They had only known each other a while—but they had both known that what they had was going to last. For a minute she couldn't move and squeezed her eyes together, hoping to stop the tears from appearing. She would have to stop this!

There was a lot to do and see in the town, but quite early she walked back to the hospital. She wanted to know the news. No good falling for this place if there was no job for her.

She walked into the waiting room and this time was offered tea. The other four candidates were already there and there was the usual strained atmosphere when people knew they were in competition and only one of them would be lucky. Three of them were staring at nursing magazines. The fourth—Fiona—was talking loudly to the secretary, calling her by her name at regular intervals, making it very clear that she was the internal candidate, and thus ought to be the favoured one. Jane picked up a magazine herself.

The door to the interview room opened and Paul Carrington appeared. His previously smiling face was now serious as he looked at the five pairs of eyes staring at him.

There was a moment's silence then he said, 'Mrs Wilson, the board would like to see you please.'

Silence still. Somehow Jane managed to walk to the door held open by the CAO.

'Please, sit down, Mrs Wilson.' Paul Carrington had taken his place at the centre of the interviewing panel again. 'Now, you have read the conditions of service for this position, you understand the salary offered?'

'Y-yes...I—I understand,' she stammered. She felt dazed, realising that until now she hadn't really expected this to happen. In fact, she hadn't really cared. But now it was all too real.

'Have you any questions you would like to ask us?'

'I don't think so.'

'Then we would like to offer you this post. Do you need a little time to consider?'

'No.' Suddenly she felt strong, felt confident. This was the first positive thing she had done since... Don't let the thought just trail away, face up to what you mean, she told herself. This was the first positive thing she had done since her husband had died.

'Thank you, no. I had already decided that I'd love to work here.'

'Then we're pleased to have you. I hope you'll be happy with us.' The board members came from behind the table and solemnly shook hands with her, one by one. All of them were smiling including Chris Fielding. He was looking at her—approvingly?

She had done it now. She was starting a new life.

CHAPTER TWO

IT WAS surprising and rather frightening to discover how easy it was to get rid of an old life. She had thought she was settled, but within days she had disposed of that settlement.

All her married life Jane had lived in their small flat with her husband. It was hard when she remembered the fun they had had together, choosing and buying it. And they had been so happy there! But that part of her life had to go. She was moving north.

When she went to the estate agent's she was appalled at the large amount of money she was told she'd get for the flat. 'Things have changed in the past couple of years, you're in a premium position,' the agent said. 'You'll get an offer within a week.' And she did. The buyers wanted to move in quickly, this suited her, too. There would be no time for regrets.

She sorted everything she had, asking herself what it was she really needed. A lot went to the charity shops, some things went to friends, the furniture she wanted to keep went to storage. She had a weepy evening sorting out John's clothes, books and so on. Just one or two things she kept, and then she invited two of his friends to dispose of everything that was left. It was the only way to do it. She had to make a clean break.

There was one farewell party. But for the past few years she and John hadn't seen too many friends, they had kept to themselves. They had had to. And then it was over. Was there anything so forlorn as the place you had once lived, now stripped of all the possessions that had made it home?

Finally there were just four large bags to be loaded into her car. This was her life. She set off to drive north, and made herself think of the future. It would be a new life, she would make new friends. It was strange, as she drove along the M1, how often the thoughtful face of Chris Fielding appeared before her. Well, she would be working with him. Of course she'd think about him.

It had been six weeks since she'd seen the hospital, though there had been many letters and phone calls. It was a long and tiring drive, but as she turned into the tree-lined drive she felt a sense of contentment. Perhaps she could be happy again here. The sun was out, it was a hot day. Was it always sunny here?

For the first few weeks she was going to live in the nurses' home. She reported to Security at the little gatehouse and a smiling porter gave her a key and instructions, told her where the luggage trolley was hidden. That was thoughtful of him. She parked in the nurses' car park—'be sure you stick your permit on the windscreen'—and decided not to unpack yet. She'd find her room and just sit for a while.

She unlocked the front door—security again!—and climbed to the third floor. From her room she could just see the sea. That was wonderful. It was a pleasant room, a bit without character at the moment but with pictures and flowers she could quickly make it her own. The room was *en suite*, and along the corridor was a kitchen with fridge, lockers and cooker. She'd have to buy some supplies.

She was still exploring when one of the doors along the corridor opened and there was the cheerful face of Erica Thornby. 'Hi, Jane, welcome! We're going to be neighbours. I heard you'd be arriving this afternoon— come in and have a cup of tea.'

'Now, that I would like. But what are you doing in the nurses' home? I thought you were…er, in a relationship? Living with someone?'

'I was in a relationship. Now I'm not. It was a case of… Look, come in and sit in my room a minute and I'll fetch a couple of mugs of tea.'

The two of them drank their tea. Briskly, Erica said, 'You're sure to hear the gossip so I'll tell you myself. I've split up from Martin Berry, my partner of five years. It just wasn't working, I decided not to settle for second best. The trouble is, he wants me back. In fact, he's been a bit of a nuisance. He'll just have to get over it. Now, d'you want me to help you with your luggage?'

'I'd like that,' said Jane. 'And the tea was more than welcome.'

An hour later she was installed in her room. The drawers and wardrobe were filled. There were pictures on the wall, a couple of photographs on her table, her own scarlet and black Navaho blanket tossed across the bed as a throw. The radio burbled quietly. The room had become a home. She was going to be happy here.

Technically, Jane started work the next day. But she wasn't allowed straight onto the ward. There was a

long interview with the administrative section, forms
to fill in, decisions to be made. She was too young to
bother about her pension! But she knew it was necessary. Then there was a one-day induction course run
by Fay Donahue, the human resources officer, where
the hospital protocols were explained to her. This she
found very useful.

Finally there was an interview with Paul Carrington.
He was as pleasant as she remembered. They sat in his
office and drank coffee.

'I did tell you that morale in the unit is rather low,'
he said. 'Of course, it's because of the amalgamation.
People are naturally a bit unsure, a bit afraid. I'm hoping you can do something about that. Individually, I
know we've got a team of excellent nurses and ancillary staff. They're good at their work and proud of it.
They just need pulling together. Chris does what he
can, but I see this as a nursing not a medical problem.'

'I agree. And I'll do what I can to build bridges.'

'Good. There is one last thing, Jane. You're entitled
to a budget—and I'm afraid it has been cut. For a long
time we've made up for missing staff by hiring agency
nurses and, of course, they cost a fortune. I'm afraid
that in future there just won't be the money for them.'

'Great,' said Jane.

On the third day she started her job proper. She had
to run the ward and manage the unit. As she walked
across the grass towards the building, she felt a little
uneasy. Still, her new uniform gave her confidence and
she was quietly proud of the signs that showed she
was Ward Manager. She had earned them.

At her old hospital she had been a sister. But she
had worked up to the position gradually, she'd known

everyone, nursing and medical and support staff. She'd known their strengths, their weaknesses. Here she was being thrown into a unit that was divided and rather hostile. Apart from Erica, she knew no one. Well, she'd just have to cope.

She arrived half an hour before handover and told the sister in charge that she was to carry on as usual. However, when both shifts were together she'd like just five minutes to introduce herself.

One of the first people she saw was Fiona Law. She looked older when wearing uniform, her long blonde hair very properly tucked into her cap. Fiona came over to her, shook hands and congratulated her. 'I hope you'll be happy with us,' she said. But Jane thought there was a coldness in her eyes.

The two shifts collected in the nurses' room, the night shift weary after their ten hours, the morning shift not yet quite awake. Jane could feel no actual hostility but neither was there any great pleasure at seeing her. This unit was going to need a lot of work. She took a deep breath, smiled and hoped things would go well.

'My name is Jane Wilson and I'm your new ward manager. There have been a lot of changes recently with the amalgamation, I'm not going to rush in and alter things that have worked well for years. I suspect we all need a period of calm. So for a while I'll just watch and work with you. I don't want to spend all my time in the office messing with paperwork, I want and need to see our babies. In the next few days I'd like to see and talk to you all individually. Thank you. Now, are there any questions that you want to ask me?'

There was a general rustling of feet, but the first one to speak was a large, middle-aged nurse. 'I'm Anne Whittle,' she said aggressively. 'I want to know if you're going to force the new rotation system on us. It's rubbish, and I for one am not going to put up with it. The other hospital was much better for us.'

Jane recognised the tone, knew that the last thing she should do was back away. Starting mildly, she said, 'I know nothing yet of the new rotation system so I can't comment on it. Perhaps you'd like to come and see me about it and explain. If I can help, I will. In general, I'm not going to force anyone to do anything. If you really don't like the conditions here, we'll just have to see about a transfer.'

She heard the intake of breath, saw the sudden whiteness of Anne's face. 'You're not going to transfer me,' she said.

'I hope not. The happiness of my staff here will be my second chief concern. My first concern will always be the welfare of our young charges.' She knew her voice had altered, hardened. Well, good. 'Let me make it quite clear. The welfare of our charges is all-important and nothing and no one will be allowed to interfere with that. I'm sure you all agree with me.' In a more gentle tone she added, 'Let me also say that I intend to do my fair share of unpopular shifts. Thank you.'

After that, handover progressed as normal. She shook hands with all the disappearing staff and tried to remember their names. She told Anne that she'd look at the rotation and come in specially that night to talk to her about it. Then it was time to start work properly.

The first job always was to walk through the wards
and check up on each of her tiny charges. She wasn't
doing the nurse's job, she was just seeing that it was
done properly. Then she went to the room that had
been allocated to her and winced at the size of the pile
of paper in her in-tray. Well, it had to be faced. She'd
start by looking at the details of the rotation system
that was causing so much ill feeling.

After an hour there was a knock on her door and to
her surprise Chris Fielding entered. It was the first time
she had seen him since the interview and his appear-
ance gave her a shock, made her catch her breath.

It was always warm in the unit—neonates lost heat
far quicker than full-term babies—and he had left off
his jacket. He was dressed in a pristine white shirt with
a dark blue tie and lightweight fawn trousers. Now
Jane could see the muscles in his arms and shoulders,
the trimness of his waist.

'I've come to add my own small welcome to you,
Jane,' he said. 'May I say that I think the board has
made the right decision.'

Somehow he seemed different, bigger. Perhaps that
was because her room was so small. She felt a shiver
of some kind of apprehension.

'You're not expected on your round yet, Mr
Fielding,' she said.

'Please, call me Chris. Just a couple of things I
wanted to check up on, there's no need for you to
come round with me.'

He moved further into the room and shut the door
behind him. 'In fact, I have a confession to make. I
eavesdropped when you were talking to the nurses. I

was very impressed. I couldn't have spoken to Anne Whittle like that.'

Jane sighed. 'I didn't want to do it. There might be things I don't know about, I need to find them out. Nurses are people, too, don't forget, they're not machines. I spoke to Anne the way I did because it's important that we know straight away where we stand. If she wants a fight she can have one. But I'd much prefer to sort things out quietly.'

'Quite so. Usually you get more with a smile than a threat.' He turned and reached for the doorhandle. 'We'll meet later on my round.'

'See you then, Chris,' she said.

He left and she went back to her paperwork, but it was a while before she could concentrate. Chris Fielding unsettled her, just by standing and talking, just by being close, he unsettled her. This was ridiculous!

Jane went back to her paperwork, checked the rotation that was causing so much grief. She looked back over the records of staffing for both hospitals and eventually groaned as she realised what had happened. Some shifts—often night shifts—were very unpopular. But working nights was part of a nurse's job. The ward managers of both hospitals had got into the habit of hiring agency staff to cover many of the night shifts. The full-time staff expected only to work days. Now that there was no money to pay for agency staff, the full-time staff had been asked to work at night. And many of them hated it. Jane sighed. It was a problem. She'd have to deal with it somehow.

Later that morning Chris came for his ward round. With him was his SHO, senior house officer. He was a tall, thin, smiling, older man called Matt Kershaw. There were quick introductions, a look at the day's reports and then Jane led the way to the wards. The first thing she noticed was Fiona. Her hair was now loosed from under her cap and flowed down to her shoulders. It looked rather nice but it wouldn't do.

'Nurse Law, go out of the ward and put your hair back up, please.' Jane didn't try to be friendly. Fiona should have known.

'Sorry, Sister. I'll do it at once.'

Jane thought that Fiona's humble tone was a little forced. And Chris paid no attention whatsoever.

It was the first time Jane had worked with Chris and she liked it. She knew he was a thorough, expert doctor. More than that, he liked his little charges. Not all doctors did. It was the usual ward round, the kind she had done so many times before. Chris and Matt would look at a baby's notes. Then, if she was handy, Chris would ask the nurse working with the baby what her opinion was. Then Matt would perform a quick examination and they'd discuss what he'd found. Jane noticed that Chris tried to involve everyone but that he always made the final decision.

'I think baby Smith here doesn't need intensive care for much longer,' he said after they'd examined the last of their charges. 'He can probably go home in a week or so. Have you seen much of his parents, Jane?'

'I've checked with the nurses. His father has been here every day, he'll be along shortly. He's devoted. But the mother is still very ill—she suffered from eclampsia and there have been some complications.'

'So sending the baby home is not an option yet?'

'The husband will do what he can. But he has to work and…'

Chris nodded. 'I'd like to talk to him again myself. See what we can sort out. Will you find out when he'll be in tomorrow?'

'I'll see to it.' She wasn't a bit surprised to discover just what a caring man Chris could be.

After the ward round they had a few more words in her room and then he stepped into the corridor. A voice called him, 'Chris? Oh, Chris?' Jane leaned back in her chair to see that it was Fiona.

Steps rattled down the corridor and then Fiona was outside, talking to Chris. Her brother-in-law.

'Looking forward to babysitting for you tonight,' she said. 'I've been thinking, it'd be more sense if I stayed the night.'

Chris's voice was even. 'It's good of you to babysit, but there's no need for you to stay. I'll happily get you a taxi. You staying would only mean more work for Mrs Mansell.'

'I won't make work. I—'

'It'll be easier to take you back,' said Chris. There was finality in his voice and Fiona didn't argue further.

It was a hard day. More staff that Jane didn't know came in for the afternoon shift and she repeated her little message. It went better this time. Then it was back to the paperwork to wrestle with the problem of rotation. And every hour she went for a ten-minute walk around her little empire. She needed to get the feel of the place and the staff. And if a parent wanted to talk to her for half an hour, well, that was part of her job.

She left late. She was tired but reasonably happy. On the whole her nurses were good and she'd established a fair relationship with the medical staff. With Chris, that is. And with his SHO. They would all work well together. She was quite looking forward to their round with her tomorrow.

When she went upstairs in the nurses' home she found an obviously upset Erica staring at her tightly clutched mobile phone. 'Problems?' Jane asked.

'My ex just won't let go,' Erica said, 'and I'm letting him get to me. But that means he's winning. Now I'm going to be strong.' She managed to smile at Jane. 'You're the one who's been in trouble. How did your first day go?'

'It went, but at times it was a bit wearying. I know I'm going to enjoy it.' She thought for a minute and then went on, 'Look, I've got an idea. You helped me settle in when I got here and I never thanked you. And I still haven't celebrated getting this job. Why don't we go for a meal together? My treat. I gather there's a place quite close to here where a lot of the staff go—the Escott Arms?'

'It's great,' said Erica, visibly cheering up. 'A bit pricy but the food's wonderful and we can walk there and back. Look, we'll go halves and I—'

'My celebration, I pay,' said Jane. 'Now, go and change and I'll call for you in an hour.'

Jane went to her room and had a bath. It struck her that her life was changing, she hadn't been out to a casual dinner like this in years. And she was looking forward to it. She found a summer dress she hadn't worn for a while and a pair of white heels to go with it. She brushed her hair, put on her usual minimal make-up. Then she went to call for Erica.

Erica, too, had obviously made an effort. Her dress was a creamy white, which went well with her dark hair and complexion. She had made up carefully, too. 'We're a couple of gorgeous girls,' she told Jane. 'Let's get in there and turn a few heads.'

'Not quite my scene,' Jane said.

She liked the Escott Arms. It was both pub and restaurant, an old house, carefully converted, with much of the original panelling and plasterwork left in place. They were shown to a banquette where they could see into the gardens at the back. It was still warm out, they were glad of the air-conditioning.

Jane ordered a bottle of chilled white wine, and for a moment they just sat and smiled at each other. 'It's good to relax,' said Jane. 'I seem to have been in a hurry ever day for the past—'

'Good Lord! It's the top nursing rank of SCBU.'

Jane looked up. There, smiling cheerfully at them, was Matt Kershaw—the rangy SHO she had been introduced to earlier that day.

'Hi, Matt,' said Erica. 'You could join us but we're having a girls' night out and doing down the entire male race.'

'Wouldn't want to spoil your fun. Also, I've just been bleeped. My presence is required.'

'Anything urgent?' Jane asked. 'Anything that I should know?'

'You're off duty,' Matt said firmly. 'I know you've done more than your fair share today. Whatever it is, it'll last till tomorrow. Enjoy your drink. One day I will join you.' And he was gone.

'Nice, isn't he?' Erica asked. 'You know he was a nurse before he became a doctor? It means he knows what we nurses have to go through, he's got a feeling for us.'

'That's good.'

'He's a good man. He lives with his father, looks after him, so no time for a social life.'

'I know the feeling.'

Erica looked at her curiously. 'You said you were a widow. You must have had a social life some time?'

Jane smiled sadly. 'I was married, I loved my husband and he died. Now I'm looking for a new life—but a professional one.'

'Not a new man?'

Jane shook her head. 'No. That side of me is dead. I was so happy at first. It just isn't worth the risk to be made so miserable again. I just couldn't take it.'

'Life is full of chances,' Erica said cryptically. 'You never know what might be round the corner. But at least it means you should get on with Chris Fielding.'

Jane was curious. 'Why so? He seems OK—a bit quiet, though.'

'He is OK. He was married…probably still is married and— Look at this!'

In front of each of them was placed a crab salad. 'It looks good,' said Jane. 'In fact, it looks fantastic.'

It tasted as good as it looked. They didn't talk through most of it, or through most of the next course either. Jane opted for fish again—it seemed silly to do anything else at this fishing port—but Erica had a steak.

Only when they were spooning up ice cream did

they start to talk again. 'You say that Chris is married?'

'Yes,' said Erica. 'Or perhaps it's a case of was married now. He was married to an archaeologist—apparently she was stunning. They had a baby and then the wife left.'

'Left? With another man?'

'Possibly. But if it was, it wasn't a local man.'

'Why? Was he a bad husband?'

Erica shrugged. 'Who knows? There's a lot goes on that we don't know about. He just doesn't talk about it, he's got a lot on his mind. But fundamentally he's a kind man.'

'Perhaps he misses the baby.'

Erica grinned. 'Hardly. He's a little boy, Chris still has him.'

Then Jane remembered the conversation between Chris and Fiona about babysitting. She had thought that Chris would be going out with his wife. 'Is the baby…all right?' she asked. 'Nothing wrong with him?' She knew there were cases—though very rare—where a mother just could not cope with a baby's apparent imperfections.

Erica shook her head. 'Nothing wrong at all. In fact, rather a nice little lad. I've seen him.'

'It's hard to believe,' Jane said. 'And so presumably Fiona is his wife's sister?'

'Ah. Our Fiona. Yes, she is the wife's sister. Watch her, Jane, she's upset that she didn't get your job—and if she had I'd have left at once. She also fancies Chris, but he seems to be keeping his distance. Perhaps, having had one sister, he doesn't want a repeat. In fact, he seems to keep his distance from all women, though I suspect he's had a few offers.'

'I see,' said Jane. 'I must say I tend to agree with you about Fiona, but I'm quite taken by Chris. He sees me as what I am, a good nurse.'

'Is that all you think you are? You are in a bad way.'

CHAPTER THREE

JANE now knew better than to spend all her time working. She worked hard, of course, but every day she put aside some time for a walk into town. It was so different from London and she liked it. After a week she was saying hello to half a dozen people, not members of the hospital but who seemed pleased to see her anyhow. And she was relaxing more. She was just thinking that there might be more to life than work.

It was Saturday, a day off, she'd been here a week. Time was flying by. In the afternoon she wandered down towards the harbour and, purely by chance, stopped to look in the window of an estate agent.

Vaguely she looked at flats—she did not intend to stay in the nurses' home for ever. She blinked at the difference in price between what she had received for her old flat and what she could buy one for here. She could afford luxury! Then she remembered buying the flat in London nine years ago when she'd been only nineteen, the joy of having their first home together, and it happened again. It didn't so often now, but the memory was always there, hiding. Tears flooded her eyes. She had been with John only ten years. It hadn't been enough.

A voice she recognised said, 'It can't be the bitter wind bringing tears to your eyes, Jane. Today is warm.'

She turned. Behind her was Chris, holding the hand

of a little boy. Just for once she didn't want to fight, to be tough. She would tell him the truth and let him make of it what he wanted.

She said, 'I was looking at flats. I'm going to buy one eventually. And I couldn't help remembering the flat I've just sold, the one where my husband died.'

'I can see that must be traumatic. You have my sympathy.'

She was glad he didn't try to over-sympathise. But she felt his comment was sincere. For a moment she felt formal so she went on, 'Don't worry, it won't affect my work.'

'I never thought it would. I see you as the absolute professional. Now, can we be friends again?' He put his hand behind the little boy and urged him forward. 'Jane, I'd like you to meet James. James, this is Jane, a lady I work with.'

Jane knelt to take the little boy's hand. 'Hello, James, I'm very pleased to meet you.'

'Hello, Jane.' She fell for him at once. His face had none of the reserve of his father, none of the abstracted air. His eyes were a different colour, too, a deep, dark brown, not like the steely grey of his father.

She stood again and said softly, 'If I say he's a lovely little boy, will you believe me?'

There was a smile. 'Of course. Remember, fathers can dote as well as mothers. And I dote on James. Not that I'm going to tell him so.'

'Of course not,' she said, and wondered if he detected the irony in her voice.

He took out a large white handkerchief and offered it to her. 'At the moment you look a bit of a mess. Dry your eyes, come down onto the harbour wall with us and I'll buy us all some of the best ice cream in town.' He paused. 'If you've got time, that is.'

'I do have time! And I love ice cream and I've never had it by the harbour. And thanks for the handkerchief.'

He led her to an outdoor café overlooking the harbour and James went to play on a little roundabout nearby. They sat in the sun and Jane thought this was all rather pleasant.

'Nothing would persuade me to order it for myself,' he said, 'but those who are less easily embarrassed tell me that the knickerbocker glory here is the best on the east coast. May I get you one?'

She giggled. 'It feels like going back to my teens but, yes, I'd love one. What will James have?'

'James thinks that ice cream is the base on which you can pour chocolate sauce, raspberry sauce, chopped nuts and hundreds and thousands. But for the moment he's happy on the roundabout. I'll order for us all and he'll come when he's ready.'

There was silence as she dipped her long spoon into the tall multi-coloured ice cream concoction and watched him eat his simple vanilla. And after a while he said, 'Talking helps, you know. I'm sure you agree that one of the most important jobs of a paediatrician—or a paediatric nurse—is offering what comfort they can to parents. Parents are often horrified when they find that the child they had so many hopes for might be gravely ill—or indeed be in danger of dying. Talking to them is a part of the job that I hate—but I would never ask anyone else to do it. However... would you like to talk to me?'

This sudden offer amazed her. 'Talk to you? What about? Why should I?'

Chris shrugged. 'I may be wrong, but I think I can see the signs. You've been bottling things up for too long. You think you've got your life on an even keel again, that you're starting a new life and the past is behind you. But it's not. Jane, I know. The past is always with you. It won't disappear. You need to bring it out, to face it, to talk about it.'

'Talk to you as to a doctor?'

He thought for a minute. 'If you wish. Or as friend. I'm not going to offer you advice. I'm just going to listen.'

Suddenly it sounded a very good idea. But…she had only been here for a few days. And for so long she had got into the habit of keeping her feelings to herself. If you told people your problems, you were vulnerable.

'It's good of you to offer,' she said, 'and perhaps some day—'

Her sentence was never finished. From behind them they heard the sound of glass breaking, then a small wail. 'Oh, Martin, are you all right?' they heard a woman call, her voice upset but under control. Then, a second later, the same voice screamed. 'Martin! Please, someone, help me, he's bleeding, he's bleeding!'

Quickly, Chris stood. 'Will you keep an eye on James for me? Sounds like someone might need help.'

'Be as long as it takes,' Jane said. 'I'll look after him, we'll be fine. And remember, I've had time in A and E.'

But even though she'd had experience of emergencies before, there was something very disturbing about the woman's now hysterical cries and the crowd that was rushing—to help or to look? Perhaps it was the contrast with the sunny day, the cheerful holidaymakers. Jane heard Chris's raised voice. 'Please, let me through. I'm a doctor, that child might need help.' Shortly after that the woman's shrieks turned into a steady sobbing, and Jane could dimly hear Chris giving orders.

Looking after James was something she could do. Her first reaction was like Chris's, to run to the scene. But then she realised it wasn't necessary. Chris knew she was here. If needed, he'd send for her. Her job was to look after James.

James was now standing beside the little roundabout, looking curiously at the crowd. Jane realised he had seen his father run to the scene and was now ready to follow him.

She walked over to him, took him firmly by the hand and said, 'Daddy says that you've to stay here with me a while and eat your ice cream. Now, I've not got any chocolate sauce—do you think I could have a bit of yours?'

James stood, obviously torn between the attractions of seeing what was happening in the crowd and eating his ice cream. 'All right,' he said, 'and you can have some red sauce as well.'

Jane led him back to the table. However, even though he shared his sauce and started to eat his ice cream, his eyes kept on darting anxiously towards the crowd. Where was his daddy? Jane knew she'd have to amuse him somehow.

She took off one of her earrings, a circle of silver

with fine silver mesh inside and a tiny sliver of blue stone hanging from it. 'Do you like this, James?' she asked. 'It's called a dream-catcher. I bought it from some Native Americans, they said that it would catch whatever I wanted.'

'You've seen some real Native Americans? And cowboys?'

Now she had all his attention. 'I went to America with my...with someone a few years ago. We saw a lot of cowboys, and we went to a rodeo.'

'Where they jump off horses onto big bulls and things? I'd like to see that.'

'It's very exciting,' Jane said, remembering how very dangerous it had looked.

'I brought back a big red and black blanket with patterns on. Right now it's on my bed, but you can wrap it round you if you're by the campfire and you're cold.'

'You shouldn't be cold by the campfire. But...can I see it some time?'

'I'll lend it to you,' she promised. 'Do you ever go to barbecues?'

'We've got one in the back garden. Daddy sometimes does sausages and bacon and things.'

A harassed-looking man in the white clothes of a cook came to their table. 'Miss Wilson? Dr Fielding says he doesn't want to leave the child until the ambulance comes. He says would you like to take James for a walk along the jetty for a few minutes? He'll find you there.'

'What's wrong with the child?' she asked.

The cook shuddered. 'Just one of those things. Dropped his bottle of orange and it broke. Then he fell on top of one of the fragments and it cut right along an artery in his arm. There's blood everywhere, I'm so glad the doctor was nearby.'

'Tell him we're fine and we're going for that walk,' Jane said.

James was happy to walk along the jetty, he liked looking at the boats. Jane held his hand tightly and they talked about cowboys. And she remembered something else she had brought back. John had bought it as a joke in Arizona, intending to give it to a nurse friend who worked on his ward and who went line dancing in boots and a large white Stetson hat. 'I've also got a keyring with a little cowboy gun on it,' she said.

James's eyes grew wide. 'I haven't got any keys,' he said.

'Panic over,' a voice said behind them. 'Have you and Jane been having a good time, James?'

She turned to look at Chris. He had pulled his jacket across his chest, but she could see blood stains on his white T-shirt. He was unsmiling and there were little pain lines by his eyes. 'How's the little boy?' she asked.

'He'll survive. Probably someone else could have done what I did, but I was glad I was there. The paramedics are good and the ambulance will take him straight to A and E. I phoned to let them know what to expect.'

'Daddy, Daddy, Jane's seen some cowboys and she's got this blanket and this gun on a keyring.'

'I see you know the way to a little boy's heart,' he said, smiling for the first time.

'We've had fun together.' Then, bluntly, she said, 'You're upset, aren't you?'

He didn't deny it. He nodded once and then said, 'I know it's entirely selfish, but that little boy was just about James's age, and all he was doing was what he does every day. It was a little boy called Martin who fell, it could have been James. It just reminded me that…that life or happiness can be fragile.'

'I know that,' she said.

He pointed to his shirt. 'I'd better get home and change this or people will wonder. The car's at the end of the jetty. Thanks for looking after James, Jane.'

'I've really enjoyed it,' she said.

Monday morning was hard.

Jane could never get used to it. Baby Hellaby was born far too early. She was born just on thirty weeks and had a low weight even for that gestation. Her chances of survival were poor—less than one in twenty.

Chris spent half an hour talking to the anguished but quiet father. Then he left, he had other jobs to do. Baby Hellaby lay there in her incubator, occasionally giving the weakest of cries. A tiny human being, surrounded by the tubes and devices of modern technology. But everything modern technology could do had now been done. On her own, baby Hellaby had to fight or die. And it seemed that she was going to die.

The instruments connected to her—the vital signs monitor, electronic thermometer, umbilical catheter sensor—recorded but couldn't arrest her slow decline.

The father remained by the side of his baby's incubator, now apparently perfectly controlled. Jane had seen this state before, when an anguished or bereaved parent would retreat into themselves, showing neither pain nor hope. When he was offered a coffee he looked as if he didn't understand the question. Then after a while he shook his head. Jane knew his silence wasn't due to bad manners. Mr Hellaby didn't recognise the outside world. All he could see and feel was in the incubator.

Jane saw him reach inside the neck of his shirt, finger something—a cross on a chain? She decided to take a chance. 'Are you a Catholic, Mr Hellaby?'

Once again the long pause while the question got through to him. 'Not a very good one,' he muttered eventually.

'Would you like me to send for Father McKellan? I know he's in the hospital and he's a wonderful man.'

'She's not going to live, is she?'

Always the temptation was to give hope and she could see the desperate need for reassurance in his eyes. But false hope was a curse. 'You have to be strong,' she said gently. 'I'll send for Father McKellan.'

The priest came quickly, had a quick word with Jane and then went to speak to Mr Hellaby. A moment later Jane saw the two of them bending over the incubator. Father McKellan was now wearing his scapular, his robe of office. He opened a little flask he always carried with him, containing holy water. She knew what was happening. Baby Hellaby was being baptised.

After a while Father McKellan joined Jane in her office and accepted a coffee. 'There are some parts of this job I dearly love,' he said. 'Usually I love baptising children. But this part I hate.'

'Does Mr Hellaby feel any better?'

'He might be a little...comforted,' Father McKellan said after a while.

'Then you've done more good than I ever could.'

The priest left shortly afterwards. There were other claims on his time in the hospital. And an hour after that baby Hellaby died. The tiny cries stopped first and then there was the inevitable decline shown on the monitor. It was expected, it had been known it would happen. But it was still hard.

Mr Hellaby sat silently by the incubator. Then he said there was nothing more to be done and he would go to sit by his sedated wife. And Jane occupied herself with the formalities that had to be followed when there had been a death on the ward.

She knew Mr Hellaby would be back. He would want to see his baby, perhaps hold her or photograph her. He might want something to remember her by— the identification bracelet was common. This was part of nursing in a SCBU. The living had to be comforted.

Nurses weren't expected to show too much emotion, they had to be sympathetic but strong ones. And it was not at all the first child death Jane had witnessed. Still, baby Hellaby's death made her feel like crying. She sat in her room, letting the tears flow down her face.

Chris came in half an hour later. 'Baby Hellaby?' he asked.

She nodded. 'She's dead. Now there's forms to sign, things that have to be done. And I'm sitting here like a green nursing cadet, feeling that I just can't cope.'

He came over and put his arm round her, a gesture of comfort. 'Nurses always have to be able to feel,' he said, 'otherwise they're hopeless at their job.'

'Feel like this? Her father kept on looking at me. He never said anything but I know what he was thinking. He was thinking why couldn't somebody do something?'

'We do whatever is humanly possible. And that should be enough to satisfy us.' He moved his arm, looked at her critically. 'When did you last have something to eat?'

Jane couldn't take in the sudden change of subject. What was he talking about? But…she considered. 'I've been busy. I had some cereal for breakfast.'

'And it's now past three in the afternoon. Your blood sugar is way, way too low and it's affecting you. Here.' From his pocket he took a bar of chocolate, offered it to her.

'But I don't feel hungry and I don't much like—'

'This is medicine, not a treat. Eat it all. Then just sit here for a while. I'll wander round the ward.'

So she did as he said. And twenty minutes later, when he returned to her room, she felt considerably better. 'You're a better doctor than I had realised,' she said. 'Your diagnosis was exactly right. I'm improved.'

'Good. But still a bit…fragile?'

'Nurses can't afford to be fragile. We have work to do.'

'I know. And you know that you and this unit are doing an excellent job. Remember I told you, when we first met, about an incubator that somehow got cold? Risking the baby's life? I know that wouldn't happen now, and that's because of you. We lost baby Hellaby. No unit in the country could have done more for her. You should think of our cases that are successful—not the opposite.'

'It's because it all is so random,' she said. 'It makes you think that nothing is worth chancing.'

'In this life you have to take chances,' he said, 'otherwise you get nothing.'

'I gather you were having an ice cream with Chris and James on Saturday?' Fiona said to Jane two days after that.

Just the two of them were in the nurses' room, having a late-morning coffee. It had been an extra hard shift so far and they both needed a break.

Jane considered the question carefully. Fiona's voice was friendly enough but Jane thought there was an underlying edge to it. Still, no need to alienate the woman. She was a competent neonatal nurse and Jane needed those. Besides, she wasn't interested in Chris, not that way. Was she?

'We just met by the harbour,' she said casually. 'I talked to James and they invited me to have an ice cream with them.'

'He's a good man, he's suffered a lot,' said Fiona. 'You know he was married to my sister?'

'I heard something about it. But I thought he still was married. Still, it's no concern of mine.'

'Of course not.'

Jane was trying to speak as if this conversation was just a casual one. but she was aware that Fiona was following her every word.

'I know you don't want gossip,' Fiona went on, 'and I certainly don't. But Chris and I have an…understanding. Nothing official. We don't want people wondering, interfering with our work here together. I've known him for a long time—longer than my sister, in fact. We're close. Very close. I just thought you ought to know since you've only just got here.'

Jane was fed up with this hinting. She'd had a hard morning's book work, and wasn't in the mood for messing about. 'Are you saying you're going to get married?' she asked bluntly.

Fiona gave a little shrill laugh. 'Oh, no. At least, not yet. There's nothing as…decided as that. And I suppose he is still married to my sister and being with her has rather put him off women—for the moment. We just have to show him who his friends are and see how things go.'

'Very commendable,' said Jane, 'I wish you the best of luck.' She banged her mug down in the sink. 'Now, can we get some work done?'

As she hurried back to her room it struck her that one disadvantage of living in a small town was that everyone knew your business. You couldn't be anonymous as you could in London.

Well, she'd shared an ice cream with Chris, that was all. His marital affairs were no concern of hers. Then it struck her that she found the idea of Chris and Fiona being together rather disturbing. Why?

It happened later that day. Chris came in to do an afternoon round, for once on his own.

He always came to her office first, he liked a quick glance at the notes before he saw his patients. Jane had to admit that the office was in a bit of a mess. Well, it was a small office and there was a vast amount of paperwork. But she thought she knew where everything was. Everything was in its proper pile.

That morning a baby had been brought in from Theatre. Baby Jordan had been diagnosed some days before as having IVH—intra-ventricular haemorrhage. Capillaries in her head had weakened and allowed blood to seep into the ventricles of the brain. Often this was not too serious and the problem resolved itself. But baby Jordan had been unlucky. A nurse had noticed that she'd seemed very weak and that her fontanelle had been starting to bulge. A bedside ultrascan had confirmed what had been suspected. IVH.

Chris had ordered a lumbar puncture to reduce the amount of fluid in the brain, and also medication to slow down the amount of fluid being produced. Neither had been enough. Baby Jordan was in danger of suffering hydrocephalus—what used to be called water on the brain. Chris had discussed the matter with the parents and they'd decided on an operation. A shunt had been inserted behind the baby's ear, a small tube that drained the excess fluid and led it to the abdomen where it was reabsorbed.

The operation had been a success. Once on the ward there had been an initial examination from Matt and then obs every hour. Jane had the records to hand, she knew Chris would want to inspect them. But when he came in, she couldn't find them.

She saw his face grow more and more blank as she turned over piles of paper, spilling some onto the floor and having to scrabble to pick them up again. She knew she was getting into a bit of a flap and the knowledge made her more irritated than ever. Where *were* those papers?

'It doesn't matter. I'll go see the baby on my own,' he said eventually. 'I'll leave you to your search.'

'No. I need to be there with you.'

'You can't until you find the notes. And time is important to me.'

'Time is important to me, too.'

Eventually she found the sheets, clipped in with a report she had been studying earlier. 'I must have put them there by accident,' she said.

He was calm, which made things worse. 'This is just not like you,' he said.

'It's not the kind of me I want to be,' she said.

'I could have sworn I put them in the proper place,' she told Erica later as they were sharing their usual evening cup of tea. 'I felt such a fool. And he took me for a fool, too.'

'It's not like you,' Erica agreed thoughtfully. 'I've never seen a more organised person. Are you sure it was you?'

'Who else? Only me bothers looking through the papers.'

'Was there anyone else on the shift in the room?'

'You know everyone wanders in from time to time.'

'Including Fiona?'

'Well, yes, but…' Jane grasped what Erica was suggesting. 'No, she wouldn't! Not hide notes just to irritate me.'

'How about hiding notes to make you look bad in front of Chris? You've told everyone that the paperwork is getting on top of you.'

'No, that's a silly idea. No one would be so petty.'

But she decided to keep an eye on Fiona in the future.

It was a part of the job that each year every nurse had to do a minimum number of days upgrading their skills on courses. This had been allowed to slip as previous managers had thought they'd had other priorities. But Jane thought it was important and she was going to insist that everyone do their full number of training days.

The big trouble was organising the time off. Already Jane was juggling with a workload that was too long and too few staff.

She had started the programme, having arranged for some of the staff to go on occasional day courses. Then Fiona turned up, smiling sweetly and saying she had a bit of an emergency. 'You know you've arranged for me to go to Leeds next Thursday? To go on that training day on developments in resuscitation techniques? Well, I really can't make it. Chris has asked me to babysit again and I'm sure you agree that's very important.'

Jane sat for a moment, seething. Then she decided to co-operate. She needed her staff to be happy. 'I'll see what I can do,' she said. 'But it's going to cause an awful lot of trouble.'

So she set to. She herself would have to do a night shift. She phoned round, calling in favours and trying gently to persuade. And after a couple of hours it was done. She sent Fiona a note.

She knew it had probably not been a good move. It was foolish to sacrifice herself for others, too quickly they thought they could take advantage. And Fiona was babysitting James. It was uncharitable but Jane thought that Fiona was not the babysitter she would have chosen.

It happened on Wednesday, two days later. She was in her office, the door ajar, waiting for Chris to arrive. She heard the sound of his footsteps—by now she could recognise them. And then there was the running tap of female footsteps and Fiona's breathy voice. 'Hi, Chris.'

His voice was more formal. 'Hello, Fiona. Look, I've had a bit of bad news. I've got to go to my meeting on Friday, just as originally planned, not Thursday. Don't put yourself out, but is there any chance of you babysitting then?'

'No problem at all,' Fiona trilled. 'In fact, I'll just nip in to see Jane now and tell her.'

Jane stared at her computer screen as Fiona came into the office.

There was no attempt at an apology. 'Don't bother changing the date of my course,' Fiona said, 'I'll stay with the original arrangement.'

'You will not,' said Jane.

Fiona looked at her, bewildered. 'But Chris wants me on Friday and—'

'Fiona. This is the second time you've tried to change an agreement that you originally made. After you left on Monday I spent hours rearranging the timetable just to suit you. I got people to give up what they wanted, come in unexpectedly, change their lives to fit in with yours. It just isn't possible to change it again.'

'So this is the way you look after your staff? I

thought you were on our side. I thought you were going to make things easy so—'

Chris came into the room. 'I couldn't help overhearing. This is all my fault so, Fiona, forget it, I'll make other arrangements. I should have realised how difficult it would be for you, Jane, and I do apologise. So, both of you, no problem.'

'But, Chris!' Fiona started. 'I wanted to—'

His voice was curt. 'I *said* there was no problem, Fiona. Now leave it.'

Fiona turned and left the room. There was a silence.

'I really am sorry about that,' said Chris. 'I've done some rescheduling myself and I know hard it can be.'

Jane shrugged. 'It's my job. I would like to help her, you know. I wasn't being awkward, but at this late stage I just can't do it.'

'I know. No problem.'

'So you're short of a babysitter on Friday night?' Jane asked after a while.

'I am. I have a housekeeper, Mrs Mansell, who comes in every day and is usually very happy to work an evening as well. But she's going away to visit her daughter. Don't worry, I'll find someone.'

'I'll babysit for you,' said Jane.

She wasn't sure why. The words just came out.

'You? Babysit?' His voice was surprised, which irritated her.

'Why not? I am a qualified children's nurse, you know. And I really got on with James.'

'Of course I know you're qualified. And James has asked after you several times.' He looked at her speculatively. 'Friday night? The end of the week? You're not going out?'

'No. If you've got a TV, I'll be happy. Just one thing I want to say. This is an offer to look after your child, nothing more. And will you make that very clear to Fiona? I've got to work with her.'

There was that thoughtful look again. 'I see. Jane, whatever relationships I might have are no concern of Fiona's. Still, I can see that… I'll talk to her. Jane, thank you so much. We'll make the arrangements later, OK?'

'OK,' she said. 'Now, I'm a bit concerned about baby Jordan…'

Afterwards, when he had gone, she wondered what she had done. Why had she offered to babysit to make his life easier? She didn't know him that well. And she knew that it would be bad for her relationship with Fiona. Even though Chris might explain, Fiona just wouldn't believe that Jane wasn't interested in him. She didn't need battles with her staff, especially those like Fiona who were quite competent.

But she did like James and wanted to help look after him. And…there was just a vague thrill at the thought of going to Chris's house. She would get to know him better. A house said so much about its owner's personality. And she'd like to know a bit more about Chris.

The house was not what Jane had expected. A modern detached building, the paint fresh and the garden obviously newly planted by a contractor, exactly the same as the garden next door. It was in a small new development of executive homes on the outskirts of town in a cul-de-sac. Good for children to play in. But

she had thought he might live somewhere more...
established.

She arrived at six o'clock on Friday evening, as arranged, and parked outside. In the drive was a burgundy Range Rover. Not quite the car she had antic-
ipated him having. Chris was turning out to be
different from her preconceptions.

As she walked up to the front door she felt a little
nervous. She had arranged to come early, to spend
some time with James before Chris left. She wanted
to be sure that they would get on as well as the first
time they had met. This would be for so much longer.
'You'll get on fine,' Chris had reassured her. 'I just
know you will. He liked you before.' But she still
needed to be sure.

He must have been waiting for her because he answered the door immediately she rang. It was a warm
evening and he was dressed casually in shorts and a
T-shirt. Involuntarily, she shivered. He had an athlete's
body with muscled arms, legs... They were disturbing.

'Come in. Good to see you,' he said. 'James and I
are having an iced orange juice. Would you like one?'

'I'd love one. And then I'd like you to leave me
alone with James for a while.'

'I was going to give him an early tea.'

'Let me make his tea later. It's more important that
we get to know each other first.'

'I see this is something you've done before. I've told
him you're coming. He remembers you and he's looking forward to seeing you again.' He led her to a small
room to the side of the hall. 'I'm afraid that, as ever,
James is to be found watching television,' he said as
he opened the door. 'I suppose I don't really approve

too much, but I have to admit that, like most one-parent families, it would be hard to cope without it.'

'Don't tell me, I know. I've met others in the same state.'

It was a pleasant little room, obviously James's own domain. James himself was sitting on the floor, staring intently at a cartoon. 'You go and work or something,' she murmured to Chris. 'I'll find you if I need you.'

He looked at her in silence for a moment and then said, 'I might have known you'd be as efficient at babysitting as you are at nursing. I'll just fetch your drink then I'll be in my study across the hall.' Then he was gone and she sat on the floor by James. Two minutes later a glass of iced orange was placed by her side.

She realised very quickly that James remembered her and that they were still friends. After watching the cartoon for a while, he told her about his favourite toys—Thomas the Tank Engine and his friends. There was a chart of the engines on the wall, and slightly to her surprise he could name all of them. Then they looked through his collection of books.

After half an hour she crossed the hall and looked around the half-open door of the study. It was an agreeable room, a mess of papers and books, with a battered desk and a very comfortable-looking leather chair.

'I think we're going to get on,' she told him. 'You can go when you like. I'll do his tea now. Do you want any?'

Chris shook his head. 'No, thanks, there'll be a buffet at this conference. But come along here and I'll show you what I've got ready for you and James.'

He took her to a modern kitchen, all strip lighting

and expensive pine-panelled units. Although luxurious, it seemed rather bare to her. The only personal touches were drawings by James, pinned along the wooden surfaces. Well, perhaps Chris was a minimalist.

She had vaguely been aware of a humming noise coming from the kitchen, which had now stopped. The washing machine. Chris pulled out a large plastic basket and began to unload it. 'Mrs Mansell does all my ironing,' he explained, 'but I can manage the washing. This will wait till she comes back. Now, I've prepared tea for you both.' He pointed to a side table where a white cloth covered food for James and her. 'There's a bottle of red wine there as well,' he said, 'and in the fridge a bottle of white. I hope you'll have a drink. And don't worry about getting home—I'll take you myself or phone a taxi for you.'

'I might have just a small one. But I tend not to drink too much on my own.'

'Probably a good idea.' He looked at her thoughtfully. 'A personal question. When your husband was very ill—when you in effect were sitting on your own—were you tempted then just to have one drink? And then perhaps another?'

'It is a personal question,' she said, 'but I'll answer it. Yes, I was tempted and once, perhaps, I did have more than I should. But then I saw where it could lead and I never had too much again.'

It was her turn to study him. 'You know what I'm talking about, don't you? You've been tempted yourself.'

He waited a moment but then answered honestly. 'Yes, I've been tempted. With me it took till the second occasion before I realised what might happen. But that was quite a while ago.'

Jane managed not to smile. He obviously didn't want to talk further about his own faults. He went on, 'Now, about payment—'

She interrupted him. 'If you say any more I shall be insulted. I don't want to be paid, I'm doing this because I choose to and I want to.' After a moment she added, 'You wouldn't expect to pay Fiona, would you?'

'No. But, then, my relationship with Fiona is different from my relationship with you.'

'Quite,' Jane said crisply, and then blushed a little as she saw the way he was smiling at her. He had guessed what she was thinking.

'Fiona is my sister-in-law,' he said gently. 'And, I hope, a good aunt for James. But she'll never be more than that. Now...' His tone altered. 'Perhaps I'd better show you round the place so you know where everything is.'

He showed her James's bedroom, with its Thomas the Tank Engine duvet and cartoon characters on the wallpaper. Next door was the bathroom with an assortment of cheerful towels and yellow plastic ducks. As they turned she saw through an open door into what was obviously his bedroom. It was an essentially masculine room. The walls were plain, the furniture even plainer. There was a double bed with a dark blue cover and his clothes for the evening laid out neatly on it.

As they went downstairs she realised what had been nagging at her subconscious. This was a very pleasant house but it was no one's home. Apart from James's two rooms and Chris's study, there was no sign of anyone trying to put their mark on this house. There were no knick-knacks, no pictures, no personal items that made a place seem personal. It was almost sterile.

'Have you lived here long?' she asked.

'A couple of years. The attraction of this house is that it's efficient. I've got a bigger, older house with a great garden, but running it on my own got too much for me. I've had to let it but I'd like to move back some day.' He paused and then said, 'You've heard that my wife and I have parted?'

'I try not to listen to gossip but, yes, I did hear. Have you parted for good?'

'Absolutely. I did have hopes for a time…but they're over now.'

There was silence for a minute and then she said, 'But you seem to be doing a good job of looking after James on your own. He seems a well-balanced little lad.'

'I do what I can. But I've always believed every child needed two parents. Now, if you'll excuse me, I'll go and get changed.'

Interesting, she thought.

James was now ready for his tea and together they went to see what Chris had put out. Jane was agreeably surprised. There was salad, cold ham and chicken, and a plate of fruit. There were also rolls which had obviously been bought that afternoon.

She made a pot of tea for herself and then they ate at the kitchen table. James was a good companion, they talked and laughed together. She wondered if perhaps she spent too much time with ill children—it was good to remember how pleasant the company of a well child could be.

It was quite a surprise when she looked up to see Chris in the doorway. Now he looked very much the professional. She knew that he was driving over to York University to meet other academics. He wore a dark suit in some lightweight material, a pure white shirt and a college tie. She thought he looked good— but she had preferred him in the shorts and T-shirt. Not that she cared very much either way, she told herself.

'Glad to see everyone enjoying themselves,' he said, and stole a bite of James's ham and salad sandwich. Then he hugged and kissed his son. 'I'll see you in the morning, James. I know you'll be a good boy and look after Jane.'

Then he took her to one side and gruffly said, 'You've got my mobile number. I'll keep it switched on just in case. But I know you'll not need to phone. Jane, there's no one I'd rather leave James with.' Then he was gone.

That was rather a nice compliment, she thought. She'd noticed that Chris always told the truth. Unlike some doctors she had met, he didn't try to hide hard facts from the parents of his patients—he felt that the truth was better faced early on. When he'd said that there was no one he would rather leave James with, he'd meant it. And that meant he'd rather leave James with her than with Fiona. The thought pleased her.

After his tea James was feeling tired. He'd had a long day and it had been warm. So she took him upstairs for his bath, watched him clean his teeth and put on his Thomas the Tank Engine pyjamas. He went to bed willingly—for which she was grateful. Then they chatted for a couple of minutes about cowboys and her trip to America. Then she read him a story and almost instantly he was asleep.

She connected the child alarm and quietly closed his door. That was the easiest bit of babysitting I've ever done, she thought.

She couldn't resist the temptation. Chris's bedroom door was still open and she peered round it. As neat and tidy as before. The clothes he had discarded had been put away somewhere. There was hardly a sign that a man slept here, lived much of his life here, read in bed, perhaps drank tea, perhaps stared at the ceiling in the dark and wondered where his life was going. The place was sterile and reminded her of an operating theatre. Could a room look lonely? She thought of her own little room, with a little effort so easily made comfortable and homely. If this bedroom were hers, she would... Jane turned and went downstairs.

She had brought herself a book and a couple of magazines. She flicked through them then discarded them. There was a TV in the living room but no programme she particularly wanted to watch. She felt restless—unusual as she'd had a hard week.

She went to the kitchen, made herself another cup of tea but decided she didn't really want it. Then she saw the basket of still slightly damp washing that Chris had pulled out of the machine. She wondered. Could she? Should she? Would Mrs Mansell mind? Would Chris mind?

She knew she was unusual but she quite liked ironing. It occupied mind and body without really stretching either. So she found the iron and ironing board and started. And, as ever, once she was in the rhythm, it calmed her down. But it was an odd feeling, ironing a stranger's clothes. It was curiously intimate.

When she finished the basket of clothes she felt quite warm. She washed her face in the downstairs bathroom, made herself a cup of tea and this time drank it. She went twice to check up on James. She sat and tried to read one of her magazines. Then she got up and opened the bottle of red wine, poured herself a glass. It was a good wine, she enjoyed it. But she promised herself that she'd only have one glass. Why was she so restless?

She thought of this house—what did it remind her of? She decided it was like the rooms in the nurses' home—like her room before she'd impressed it with her own personality. This house was pleasant, comfortable, but anonymous. Either Chris didn't know how or he had deliberately decided not to personalise this place. She wondered if the older house he owned showed anything about him. Or did it show something about his wife—or ex-wife?

This place was deliberately being left without what might be called the woman's touch. She thought that the two of them had something in common, both of their lives had been turned upside down. But they had reacted in different ways. She shrugged, it was a stupid idea. Then she went to make herself yet another cup of tea.

Jane was dozing a little when lights flashed through the window. She checked her watch—half past twelve. About the time Chris had said he'd be back. She went into the kitchen to put on the kettle, he'd want a drink.

Then she went into the hall to greet him. 'Good meeting?'

He was tired, she could tell by his eyes. But he smiled and said, 'A very good meeting. A small firm has developed a new apnoea monitor which appears to be superior to all the others. I was impressed. Trials are still running, but I can see us ordering a couple quite soon.'

An apnoea monitor warned the staff when a baby's breathing was too shallow or too slow. It was an important piece of equipment.

'James has been fine,' she told him, 'sleeping like a little lad who's had a hard day. Now I'll make you some tea, and would you like a sandwich? You left us no end of food.'

'Tea would be most welcome but I think I've had more than enough to eat. But let me get it, I—'

'You've done enough, you looked tired. And I've been half-asleep. I'll do it.'

He followed her into the kitchen, watched her as she made the tea. He took off his jacket and tie, rolled up his shirtsleeves. Then they sat in the little alcove, facing each other. He was absent-mindedly rubbing his forearms, his fingertips catching on the fine hair. She found the movement curiously exciting. Then he looked at the far end of the kitchen and saw the piles of ironing. 'Jane? Did you do that ironing?'

She blushed a little. 'I like ironing. I find it soothing.'

'But you're here to look after James, you're not a—'

'I enjoyed it,' she said. 'Chris, I really did.'

'You're a woman in a thousand,' he said. 'But

didn't you find ironing a stranger's clothes a bit—well, unusual?'

'Are we strangers, Chris?'

'No,' he said after a while, 'not any more.' Then he drank his tea in silence. Afterwards he looked around him, saw the opened bottle of red wine. 'You didn't have much to drink,' he said. 'Didn't you like it?'

'It was gorgeous, heavy and oaky and with lots of tannin. Just how I like it. But I thought we agreed that drinking on your own wasn't a good idea.'

'You're not on your own now. Shall we go into the living room, sit down and have a glass each?'

'All right,' she said, after a pause.

He picked up the bottle, reached into a cupboard for a couple of glasses. Then he led her to the living room, flicked on a table lamp. She sat on a black leather couch. Rather to her surprise, he sat by her side, put glasses and bottle on the coffee-table in front of them. He poured them a glass each, lifted his to toast her. 'Here's to…what?' he asked.

She thought a minute. 'Long life and happiness?'

'That's as good as anything. All we need now is to know how to get them.'

'Sounds a serious subject for this late at night.'

'True. We'll talk about something else. You've been here four weeks now, how're you settling in? What's it like here, after London?'

They could talk about work, this was easy for her. 'I'm settling in and I'm enjoying the work—though there's a lot of it. But I can see an end to it. In time we'll have a happy, efficient department, delivering a good service to the community.'

His voice was soft. 'That is good. But what's in it

for you, Jane? Are you happy, finding fulfilment? I mean, in your personal life.'

They were on dangerous ground again, she didn't like talking about her feelings. So she said neutrally, 'Well, I must start looking for a flat soon. I've made some friends, I expect I'll have more of a social life later. I told you, I got used to living on my own when I had John to look after. We were enough for each other. And it's a bit hard for me to get out of that pattern.'

'I know what you mean.'

She was relaxing now. It was good to half sit, half lie there, slowly sipping the wine. And Chris was good company. She was enjoying talking to him.

She guessed she ought to be tired. She'd had a long day. In fact, she'd had a long week. But she wasn't tired, there was some other feeling that she could neither understand nor express. She felt at home with Chris. This was new. Before, he had always seemed abstracted, even though friendly. But now she'd seen him with James, looked round his home, he'd become a more approachable person.

She bent forward to put her glass on the table. When she leaned back someone must have moved because their shoulders and hips were now touching. Had he moved on the couch? Or had she?

She turned her head to look at him. There was only the dim light of one lamp and she could see the whiteness of his shirt but his face was in shadow. Time passed—seconds or hours, she did not know.

He took her hand from her lap, held it in the lightest of grips. She knew that if she wanted to she could break the grip. But she didn't want to break it. At least, not yet.

He said nothing but sat there, she knew he was staring at her face. What her face betrayed she did not know. She didn't understand her own feelings. The light was behind him so she couldn't see his face, couldn't read his feelings, so she closed her eyes. Then she felt the warmth of his breath on her face, felt his arm slip round her shoulders.

She knew this was the moment of decision. She could lean forward, reach for her glass. Whatever was between them, this fragile moment, would be broken. It could be ignored and quickly forgotten. Fearfully, she realised this was not what she wanted. Her feelings, usually so tightly under control, were betraying her.

She let her body lean into his, her arms wrapped loosely round his waist. It was the tenderest of kisses. He kissed her on the lips, tentatively, as if he was as uncertain as she was. She liked being kissed this way, for a while she was happy with it. But then, to her amazement, she discovered that this was not enough. It surged from some hidden depth deep inside her, a need, a hunger so strong that she could neither question nor evade. She needed so much more.

She put her hand round his neck, pulled him tighter to her, even opened her mouth to him. He took advantage of this offer. His kiss became deeper, harder, he took her lips, searched her mouth, making her feel more like a woman than she had felt in years. It was so good! She could feel her heart pounding in her breast, her chest heaving with excitement. She wanted this so much!

And then he drew back. The kiss ended and she felt forlorn. 'Just a kiss,' he said hoarsely, 'just a thank-you kiss. You've been so good to James and me, and I...'

She knew this was an excuse and felt a rush of mixed emotions for what he was doing for her. He was offering her a way out. They could stop now if she wanted, nothing more would be said. And for a moment she thought about stopping, of carrying on with her work, her dull but pleasant life. Her peaceful, calm and ordinary life. But she was only twenty-eight and her life needed to sparkle sometimes.

'That was more than a thank-you kiss,' she muttered. 'And we both know it. But if you want us to stop...'

He kissed her again. Now his arms were round her, easing her onto her back on the couch, looming above her as he kissed her with a desperation that she shared and revelled in. All her senses were heightened, she could smell the leather of the couch, the lemony tang of his aftershave, even the sun-warmed heat of his body. She could taste the wine on his tongue—could taste *him*. There was the sound of their bodies on the couch. And her body was a maelstrom of feelings.

There was the tightness of his arms round her, his thigh pressed to hers told of his need for her. And in response her body seemed sensitised. Her breasts were tight, almost painfully so, and her nipples were erect with excitement. A warmth shimmered from her hips, she could feel the dampness of passion. She was so happy. This would do for now. But she knew there must be more.

Eventually he eased back from her, and muttered, 'Jane, we must…'

She pulled him down to her again, kissed him firmly. 'What we must do is not talk,' she said. 'Now, where are you taking me?'

Time stretched as she gazed up at him. And then he said, 'Come to my bed.'

Arms round each other's waists, they walked upstairs. He led her to his bedroom, switched on a bedside lamp, and a light as dim as the one downstairs filled the room. The room that before had seemed so clinically sterile now seemed full of promise.

For a while they stood and kissed each other. She could sense his doubt and so she said, 'I should tell you. I've been under some stress lately and it's affected my periods a bit so my GP has prescribed progestogen. In effect, a contraceptive pill. Nothing we do will have…consequences.'

'Anything we two do will have consequences,' he said. 'But now—who cares?'

He kissed her again. Then he felt for her shirt, lifted it over her head. He undid the clip of her plain white bra, eased it down over her arms and she felt her breasts tighten even more in the cool air. Then he bent his head to kiss each aching tip and she groaned with the ecstasy of it.

She kicked off her sandals. His hands were fumbling at the waistband of her jeans, undoing the belt and sliding them down to her ankles. She was wearing the sheerest of white briefs. She felt his fingers reach inside, brush her there, and she sighed. Then she was fully naked.

He bent, slid an arm behind her knees and picked

her up, she marvelled at his strength. Reverently, he laid her on his bed, kissed her again. 'You're still dressed,' she moaned. 'Why have you got all those clothes on?'

He stepped back, she heard the rustle of his shirt as he dragged it over his head. Then he was coming to her. She stretched her arms behind her head, she would be an offering to him.

His lips were on her again. Then he was kissing her entire body, awaking in her feelings that for so long had been dormant, a fiery excitement that she thought she could hardly bear. She still knew she needed more.

'I want you now, Chris,' she panted. 'Please, Chris, I want you now.'

Then he was poised above her. The darkness of his body blotted out all thought of the past. She reached for him, clutched her to him. She knew that she was open for him, she wanted him entirely. And then that feeling, so familiar and yet so new, that feeling of gladness at being so important, at being the centre of her man's universe. And the pleasure was so great!

Whatever he was doing to her throbbed through her entire body. It was a feeling too intense to last long. Within what seemed like seconds she was responding to his crescendo of excitement, urging her writhing body to his, calling out with him at that moment of joint ecstasy. And then it was over.

'That was so good,' she murmured.

Then afterwards he got up to open a window and they lay side by side, letting the salt-scented breeze cool their damp bodies. 'Jane,' he muttered, 'I don't know what to say. That was like…like nothing I've ever felt before. But we must talk and—'

'Hush,' she cautioned. 'Certainly we must talk. We'll wake early tomorrow morning and talk then. But for now I want just to be here and sleep with you. Are you happy with that?'

'Very happy,' he said.

CHAPTER FOUR

JANE woke early. That was not her usual ceiling, for a moment she wondered where she was. Not her London flat, not the nurses' home...Chris's bedroom! What had she done?

For a moment she lay there and recaptured the night before, remembered the rapture, and for a moment allowed herself to enjoy it again. It had been so long and they went together so well—but now what?

Both of them were naked. She vaguely remembered waking in the night, feeling his hands resting on her breasts while he slept. She had pulled them to her. Now she was enjoying the warmth of their bodies together under the sheet. But she knew it couldn't go on.

Gently, she moved his arm from round her, slipped out of bed. It was early, six o'clock. She grabbed her clothes, carried them downstairs and quickly dressed. Then she made two mugs of tea and carried them back upstairs. She had to move quickly. Apart from anything else, she had to leave before James was awake.

Chris's eyes opened as she entered the room. She put his tea by his side of the bed and took her own tea to a chair on the other side of the room. Then she shut the door, she didn't want their talking to wake James.

'Aren't you coming back to bed?' he asked hopefully.

'No. It's better if I keep my distance while we talk.' Even to herself, her voice sounded abrupt.

He pulled himself upright and she saw that muscled chest, the arms that had wrapped round her and the fingers that had brought her so much pleasure. She had to steel herself against him! What she had to say wouldn't be easy.

'You look like a woman who has just made up her mind about something,' he said, 'and I suspect it's something I'm not going to like.'

Well, that was bright of him. And what she was going to say she didn't like herself. But she knew it had to be said.

'Last night,' she said. 'First of all, there's no blame on either side, we both did what we did because we wanted to. I'm a mature woman, in no way was I led astray by you.'

'Quite so,' he said quietly.

'Secondly, I don't regret a minute of what happened. It was wonderful, I loved every second.' She blushed faintly as she realised what she was saying. 'It was so good,' she ended faintly.

'It was so good for me, too. I don't think I will ever forget it.' He still spoke quietly, sadly even. 'But is there a third thing?'

'Yes. You remember at the harbour café, you asked me if I wanted to talk? About how things might get better if I talked about them?'

'I remember.'

'Well, I'll tell you now.' And as she said it she realised how lonely she must have been. This was a story that no one had heard in full.

'It's just a simple, ordinary story,' she said. 'Hospitals are full of them.'

'Most people are neither simple nor ordinary. And every story is unique in some way. Go on, tell me your story.'

'Ten years ago, I was eighteen and I started training as a nurse. I met John, he was training to be a doctor. He was four years older and we clicked just like that. A year later we got married. We had a quick honeymoon in America and then we came home and scraped together a bit of money and bought a little flat. We were both so happy. The plan was for us both to finish training, have a year or so to get established and then think about babies. John qualified. He was so proud to be a doctor, he thought in time he might become a surgeon. But first House Officer and then Senior House Officer.'

Remembering this first bit of her life with John had made her happy. But then things had changed.

'Then, three years later, it started. I remember the first time. He fell over, just stumbled. We both thought he was overtired. But then it happened again and again, so he went to see his GP. I think he already might have had a suspicion, but he said nothing to me. The GP referred him to a consultant but…it was too late.'

She knew she didn't have to go through all the details with Chris, a doctor would know.

'He had brain-stem cancer. They tried everything but, as you know, it is often inoperable. He had chemo, of course, but that didn't do much good. I can remember the hopes, the fears, the gradual, slow realisation. Nothing could be done. The last year of his life I nursed him at home, watched him die. I wanted to give up work, he insisted I shouldn't. He said I had to have a life, but I said he was my life. But because he wanted it, I went to work.'

Now the tears were running again, but she did nothing to stop them. 'I can remember the heartache when he said he knew he was going to die, and that the worst thing was knowing he was leaving me. He said he'd die happier if I promised that I'd make myself a new life when he had gone. He said… he said…to remember he'd be looking down at me.'

'He sounds a good man,' Chris said. 'And, of course, you miss him. Every day you miss him.'

'Perhaps it gets easier,' she said, 'a bit easier. For a while I forget and then it all comes back to me and I feel worse than ever.'

'I know how you feel,' he said. 'But things will improve in time. I know that myself.'

'They haven't improved yet. And I'm just terrified of the future. So you know this has to end now. There isn't, can't be any future for us. You're still married, I'm…I'm just widowed and in no way do I want the pain of another relationship. I couldn't…couldn't stand it. And don't laugh, but I'm just not into casual sex. I've only ever slept with my husband and you.'

'I'm sure of that. But if you're not into casual sex—why me?'

It was a good question and she didn't know the answer, 'It just happened,' she said. 'I know there will be no consequences but I didn't do it because of that. It was just something that suddenly I wanted.'

'I wanted it, too. And I'm not into casual sex either. I was living my life quite happily without women, but then I met you and suddenly things were different. You've been a bright light in my life, Jane.'

This conversation wasn't going the way she had expected. She had expected—hoped perhaps—that he would argue with her, try to persuade her to change her mind. And that would have strengthened her resolve. But he was just sitting there, looking upset, and that was harder to bear.

'Look, Chris, we have to work together—can't we just forget this happened? It'll be easier that way. Just never mention it again.'

'I'd find it hard to forget it happened,' he said. 'In fact, I'd find it impossible. But if you want to put it behind you, so be it. I know I have no right to object. But at least tell me why.'

'I do want to put it behind us,' she said quickly, 'and it will be best for both of us. And why is because I can see nothing but hurt in it for me.'

'You were taken by surprise,' he said. 'But then I was surprised, too. I never had any intention at all of having sex with you. And I would never hurt you.'

'It was something that we did together. Now drink your tea.'

There was silence for a moment. 'I don't want you to go,' he said. 'I want you to stay longer, we can talk things over, see what we can make of them.'

'No, Chris, I can't stay! Please, don't ask me. I'm just getting my life into some kind of balance, just getting free of the past. I can't take any more heartache. I know you say that you don't want to hurt me and you mean it. But I will get hurt, I know.'

This time the silence lasted much longer. He was looking at her and she couldn't stand the sadness in his eyes so she stared at the floor. Finally he sighed and said, 'Jane, this is a decision that only you can make. No way will I try to push you into something that you don't want. But will you at least come over here and kiss me goodbye?'

Such a temptation! But she must resist it. 'I kissed you enough last night and I'll never forget it. But now I have to go. Goodbye, Chris.' And before he could speak again she ran out of the room, hurtled down the stairs. She was terrified he might come after her and she knew that if he did he'd persuade her to stay. But a minute later she was in her car and then she was safe.

She didn't drive straight back to the nurses' home. Instead, she took the coast road, then turned onto a minor road and parked up on the cliffs.

It was still early, it would be a while before the holiday crowds flocked up here. She had the morning to herself. The air was like salt champagne and the faintest of breezes stroked her cheeks.

She walked till she stood on the very edge of the cliffs. Below her the sea was a dark blue, the sky a lighter blue, the cliffs white. A golden line of sun stretched towards her and in the distance a couple of passing ships were dark on the horizon. Everything she saw seemed clear, simple, defined. If only life were like that!

She was starting a new life here. She had planned it, thought about it, knew exactly what she needed. Last night shouldn't have happened. It had opened the way to even greater misery and she had been happy here. But she could put what had happened behind her. If she had learned one thing over the past few years, it had been how to accept and deal with bad fortune. In time all pain grew less. It had to. She would cope, she would put Chris out of her life. And if it hurt, well, she had dealt with hurt before.

She went back to her car—time to drive to the nurses' home. When she sat behind the wheel she caught the faintest of scents. She lowered her head, sniffed. Then she pulled open the front of her shirt, and there it was. Her body still smelled faintly of Chris's. And it was so exciting! And so it was forbidden. She would go home and shower at once.

It was Saturday morning, no one noticed her arrival or the fact that she had been out all night. She undressed, thrust the clothes she had discarded to the bottom of her linen basket and vowed to wash them that afternoon. Then she showered and shampooed her hair. She would wash away all traces of last night.

Until the age of eighteen her blonde hair had been long, cascading down her back like a golden stream. It had been gorgeous. But when she started nursing training she'd had it cut in a bob, so much easier to cope with. Later still, when her husband had fallen ill, she'd had it cut even shorter in an almost boyish crop. She knew it suited her. But when she'd come to this new job she had decided to let it grow out. Change of job, home, lifestyle, change of hair, too. Something more feminine. Though why she wanted to be more feminine, she did not know.

She dressed casually then went along the corridor to make herself some breakfast. She wondered if Erica was awake, they often shared a meal when they were in together. And company would be good for her. It would stop her thinking about what she had now to give up.

Erica was in the kitchen She was red-eyed, in her dressing-gown, clutching a cup of tea for comfort. Jane knew at once what had happened. 'He's been on the phone again?'

'Yes, he has. But I won't give in, I won't, I won't. I won't see him, talk to him, write to him. I'm going to be strong! You've told me that.'

'Yes, I have,' said Jane. She wondered why she couldn't take her own excellent advice.

It was good to work on the ward. Here she knew what she was doing, felt confident of her skills, enjoyed the feeling of satisfaction in helping someone otherwise so helpless.

'That new baby doesn't look too good,' Sue, one of the trainee neonatal nurses, said to her as she walked along the corridor. 'D'you think you could have a look, please?'

Jane looked at the girl's anxious face. She could remember when she herself had always been anxious, unable to believe that babies so small, so apparently feeble, could ever grow to maturity. But they did. 'I'll come along,' she said to Sue. 'But you tell me what you've observed and what possible conclusions you have drawn.'

The girl thought. 'Baby Reynolds, admitted this morning at thirty weeks. She seems to have difficulty breathing so she's probably not getting enough oxygen. She grunts a bit as she breathes and her nostrils flare out. Her skin is sort of blotchy and a bit blue in colour.'

'And this all suggests?'

'Well, it could be a lot of things so I think the first thing I should do is call a doctor. But if I had to diagnose I'd say it was RDS—respiratory distress syndrome.'

'You're right to be cautious. If you're in any doubt, always ask someone. But I suspect you're right, let's have a look.'

They peered at the tiny figure sprawled on her back in the glow of the incubator. Jane pointed at the chest. 'See how the skin and muscles are pulled in when the baby tries to breathe? Always a tell-tale sign.' Jane bleeped the doctor on call and told him her suspicions. 'Now while we wait for the doctor, can you tell me what is most likely the cause of the RDS?'

The girl had done her homework well. 'Probably a lack of surfactant,' she said. 'Surfactant is the substance which coats the inside of the alveoli, or air sacs, of the lungs and stops them collapsing inwards. This makes it hard for the baby to breathe and she may not get enough oxygen and fluid may enter the lungs. In many babies the condition is not serious and sorts itself out.'

Jane grinned to herself. 'You remember your lectures well,' she said. 'But it's different when you see an actual baby with it, isn't it?'

'It scares me,' Sue admitted. 'But I'm interested.'

The doctor, Chris's senior registrar, Joe Eliot, arrived. Jane hadn't seen too much of him but knew he was a very competent man. He examined baby Reynolds and agreed at once with the nurses' conclusions.

'Sue noticed the condition first,' Jane said. 'I'd like it if she could observe the rest of the procedure.'

'Always willing to demonstrate my skills to an admiring audience,' Joe said affably. 'Now, Sue, as it says in the television programmes—this is not something that you should try at home.'

A tube was introduced into the baby's windpipe and then an artificial surfactant, a thick fluid, was allowed to drain through it gently down into the lungs. It was a very precise and delicate operation, needing the skills of both Joe and Jane. But eventually it was done.

'This is one of medicine's little miracles,' Joe said to Sue. 'Before we had this stuff, that baby would probably have died. Doesn't it give you a warm feeling to have helped in this way?'

'You two did all the work,' Sue said. 'Watching you, I was just terrified.'

'You were part of the team and that's good. In a few years you'll be as good as Jane here. Now, set up a ventilator and we'll give baby Reynolds some extra air and oxygen, just to keep her going for a while.' Joe smiled and then said, 'Let me know if there's any alteration in her condition. Now, Jane, do I deserve an extra-strong coffee?'

'And you can raid my chocolate biscuit tin,' she said.

That had been the good part of her day. But being Ward Manager meant that there were other, less enjoyable bits to her work. Jane knew from experience how poor communication could spoil the happy working of a department. In her London hospital all too often decisions about work had been taken by some vague committee and the staff just informed by a notice or a curt note with their pay slips. This would not be Jane's way. She would talk to her staff as much as possible, find out what they felt before making any decisions and then explain those decisions in person.

It had taken some time, but now Jane thought she had worked out just what had been going wrong. She had studied the work rosters over the past few months, had consulted the union representative and got her understanding and support. Then she had devised a new rostering system.

The basic problem was that there was too much reliance on agency staff. If the unit was going to be short of a nurse, the ward sister would phone a reputable agency and arrange for a nurse to be supplied. These were always highly competent. But they cost a fortune, and they could never give the continuous support that was expected from regular staff.

It was finished with now but, from looking at the records, Jane suspected that there had been a fair amount of laxness in Princess Mary Hospital. Staff had been allowed to opt out of the very unpopular shifts, especially the night shifts at the weekend, when they could fairly have been asked to cover them. The bill for agency staff had been astronomical. And now they wanted the same conditions in the Wolds Hospital.

Jane arranged for as many of her staff to get together as was possible. She'd repeat this meeting a couple more times so that she talked to everyone, but she knew that the first meeting would be the hardest.

She explained her new system and the need for it. Her audience accepted the news gloomily. 'I know it's not going to be popular,' she finished, 'but it's necessary. And if we all pull together, I'm sure that in a few weeks it'll be working fine. Now, are there any questions?'

She might have guessed that Fiona would be the one to speak.

'I'll certainly do my best and I'm sure we all will,' she said sweetly, 'and I agree with...a lot of what you say. But it still seems that we're being asked to work a lot harder for the same salary. Look at poor Alice here. Only married six months and she's working more night shifts than ever. I do think it's wrong that you're worsening our conditions of service.'

Jane noticed that 'poor Alice' had only just realised that she had been badly treated.

'Yours is one way of looking at things,' she told Fiona evenly. She wasn't going to tell the entire group that they'd been idle and she was going to stop it. It might be true—but she wanted them to realise it themselves.

'It is going to be hard on me,' said Alice.

'Of course, we all want what is best for the unit,' said Fiona.

Jane kept her temper, she knew the last thing she needed here was a row. And, rather grimly, she had to admit that Fiona was brilliant at stirring up trouble without getting into it herself. Apparently she was sweetness and light, but attacked just enough and then let someone else carry on the fight.

It wasn't a happy meeting but in the end she got a grudging agreement that the system would be tried for six weeks. At the end of that time it would be reviewed. Jane hoped that six weeks would be long enough.

When the meeting was over she went to her own room and put on the coffee-pot. Then she started to think. She knew that one troublemaker could spoil the work of an entire group. And it was up to her to pull this unit together. She tried to put aside all personal feelings and work out what would be best.

After ten minutes she thought she had worked out a plan.

She went into the nurses' room and was lucky enough to catch Fiona there. 'Come to my room if you've got a minute,' she said, smiling. 'We can have a coffee together.'

'I'd like that,' Fiona said, smiling back.

What a pair of hypocrites, Jane thought.

'I thought you were a bit hard on my plan,' she said to Fiona when they were alone together, 'and I was wondering if there was any personal reason for your objections.'

'Certainly not,' Fiona said, trying to act surprised. 'I was only trying to put a point of view.'

Jane thought Fiona looked a little put out by this frontal attack. She decided to push harder. 'You're not upset because of any…perceived relationship between Chris Fielding and myself?'

Now Fiona was definitely rattled. 'Certainly not. As you know, Chris and I are related by marriage, we are old friends, but that's got nothing to do with—'

Jane cut in. 'It's no business of yours, but I was widowed only recently. I can assure you that the last thing I want right now is a man in my life.'

Fiona couldn't hide the spark of joy that this news gave her but said primly, 'My objections to your plans had nothing to do with your or my personal life.'

'Of course not. Do drink your coffee.' Jane leaned forward, smiled with even more saccharine sweetness than before. 'I've watched you at work, Fiona, you're a good, dedicated nurse. You do your best. The unit needs people with your skills. But let me make one thing clear. I'm not going to see one person spoil the work of the whole section. If you try to undermine me once more I'll have you out. Understand?'

Fiona looked shattered. But then she recovered. 'Of course,' she said.

Jane knew she wouldn't see Chris for the next three days. He was away on one of the many conferences that consultants had to attend. She was nerving herself for his return, not looking forward to it but knowing it had to be faced.

Then something unexpected happened.

On the afternoon of the third day, the phone rang in her office. 'Neonatal Unit, Sister Jane here.'

There was the sound of whispering. Then a small voice said, 'Jane? Is that Jane?'

She was shocked but she recognised the voice at once. 'Why, yes, it is. And you're James. How nice of you to call me.'

'I've not been very well,' the voice said. 'I've been in bed but Daddy knows and Mrs Mansell's here. Daddy's coming back late tonight.'

'James, I'm so sorry you're ill.' Then the words spilled out before she had a chance to think about them. 'Would you like me to visit you?'

'Yes, please! And could you bring the blanket to show me and perhaps the key-ring with the gun?'

'Of course I can. Now, just to arrange things, is Mrs Mansell there?'

More whispering. Then Mrs Mansell came on the line, 'He's been worrying me to call you for the past three days.' She chuckled. 'You've been telling him stories about cowboys and Indians.'

Jane laughed. 'Only about when I was in America. Is he really ill?'

'Just a bit off colour. If he'd been really ill Mr Fielding would have been back here like a shot.'

'Well, I would like to see him, but I don't want to be there when his dad comes home. I think they should have that time together.'

'Come to tea, then. Mr Fielding's not due until about ten. Can you get here about six?'

'I'll be there. Give my love to James.'

Only when she'd rung off did she start to wonder if this was a good idea.

Could she separate her feelings for James from her feelings from Chris? She had met James twice, once at the harbour and then when she'd babysat. She had been drawn to the little lad, to his seriousness, his curiosity. If she ever had a child she would like one like— She wasn't to think that way!

But he was good company. She wanted to see him. It wouldn't hurt to visit him, to take the blanket and the keyring, to have an hour with him and then be well gone by the time his father came back. It committed her to nothing with Chris, she was just visiting his son. And if there were any odd feelings about entering that house again—the one she had left so early in the morning—well, she would have to cope with them.

Still, it was a bit of a strain walking up the path and

ringing the bell. She checked first, there was no car in the drive, Chris hadn't come home early. She'd talk to James for a while and then leave well before Chris was due to come back.

She was looking forward to seeing James. She had the blanket over her shoulder, the pistol key-ring in her pocket. He'd be pleased to see her.

The door opened and there was James in dressing-gown, pyjamas and fluffy tiger slippers. His face was solemn as he looked up at her, but then he smiled. 'You've brought the blanket! I've found some pictures of Indians in my book, they're wearing blankets.' He took her hand and pulled her inside. 'Come in, I'll show you.'

In the hall was Mrs Mansell, who gave Jane a warm smile. 'He's been worrying about you no end,' she said. 'You go on into his room, I'll fetch you a nice cup of tea and then get on with some work. He has been mithering me.'

Jane went into James's room and had to sit on the floor. James had the blanket draped round him. In a corner Jane found paper, coloured pencils and sticky tape, with a bit of difficulty she constructed him a feather headdress. 'You have to have one as well,' James said, 'otherwise you're not a proper Indian.'

'Lady Indians are called squaws,' Jane said.

Mrs Mansell came in with the tea and when she had gone back through the door she was shot with the pis-tol keyring. Jane hid a smile. James knew what would be and what might not be permitted. Shooting Mrs Mansell would not be permitted.

Jane took the offered book and read a story. She

realised she was enjoying herself. She was enjoying herself being with James.

Of course, she grew to love many of her little charges. But a nurse always had to maintain a certain degree of detachment, it was the only way to remain sane. James was different, it felt as if he was…family?

She would have liked to have had a child—or two or three or four—herself, but those dreams had died with John. So why did the little boy by her side make her feel so…so…?

Jane forced herself to concentrate on the book. There was plenty of time, she kept checking her watch. After she had read the story James decided he'd like to watch one of his Thomas the Tank Engine videos. 'We can be two Indians watching our video in our tent,' he told her.

'Why not?' she asked. She put an arm round his shoulders, generously he indicated that she could share the blanket. She leaned back against a convenient arm-chair.

He had seen the video often before, and though he liked it, it had been a long day. Soon his head drooped, his eyelids flickered then closed. Jane felt perfectly content. There was the little head resting on her breasts, she could feel his warmth and the beating of his heart. Perhaps she dozed a little herself. And, un-noticed, Thomas the Tank Engine got up to his pranks.

'Well. An Indian encampment on my floor.'

Jane's eyes flew open, she looked up in horror. There was Chris looking down at them. 'What are you doing here?' she gasped. 'You're not due back for an-other couple of hours.'

'That's not much of a welcome,' he said reproachfully. 'The last session wasn't worth going to so I came back early. I wanted to chat to James before he went to sleep. But it looks like I'm too late.'

'He's been ill. He phoned. I just wanted…just wanted… He asked about my blanket and I said I'd bring it over. I wanted to see him.'

She felt at a disadvantage and was trying to disentangle herself from James without waking him. Chris crouched beside them. For a moment she caught that smell of him and there was a throb of memory, of excitement. He took James from her and sat there, holding his son.

James woke. ''Lo, Daddy,' he said, and went back to sleep.

Jane felt she had to explain. 'Mrs Mansell phoned and said that he'd been asking after me, and I knew that he wanted my blanket so I brought it and… I was coming to see him, not you.'

'Of course. James thinks you're one of his friends, he wanted to see you. I hope you'll come to see him any time you can.'

'I'd like to, but it's difficult.'

'Why should it be difficult?'

'Well, I…that is, you and I…'

Mrs Mansell put her head round the door. 'I thought I heard you come in. Two cups of tea, is it?' Obviously, for Mrs Mansell tea was the answer to all problems.

Jane scrambled to her feet. 'Not for me, Mrs Mansell. I must go now.'

'Please, stay,' Chris said. 'We could have a chat

when James is in bed. You'll be interested in the conference I went to.'

'No, I'd better go.' She lifted her hand to her head, discovered that she was still wearing her paper feathered headdress. She tore it off. 'Yes, I really must go. Thanks for the tea, Mrs Mansell, very nice. Tell James I'll see him again some time, Chris. No, don't get up, I'll see myself out.'

And then she was out of the door, driving away as quickly as she could. Not a very dignified exit.

A couple of miles from his house, she pulled off the main road and drove down a side road to where she could sit in peace and look at the green of the hills. Perhaps her rapid heartbeat would slow down here.

Of course, she had been taken by surprise. She hadn't expected him. But, still, she was shocked at the intensity of her feelings. There had been excitement, longing, he made her feel so much. But it wasn't just him. She realised she had fallen for both Chris and James. That made her feel worse. What could she do?

Perhaps she might arrange to see James on occasion—though it would be difficult. But Chris would have to be kept at a distance. They would have to revert to a purely professional relationship.

Next morning there was a knock on her office door and there Chris was. He was tall and dark-haired and wonderful and now he smiled far more than he used to. When he smiled that way at her, her stomach lurched and for a moment she was out of breath. This was stupid, she told herself. Nothing more than a physical reaction, brought on by the memory of that unfortunate night.

'How's my favourite ward manager?' he asked, 'Any chance of a cup of that wonder coffee?'

She smiled back at him thinly. 'Coffee in the percolator,' she told him. 'Help yourself. I've got a couple of jobs on the unit before you do your round.'

'No time to stop a minute and chat? By the way, James says he's sorry he went to sleep and will you call again? And may he borrow the blanket for a while?'

'Please, he can keep it. Now, help yourself to coffee. I'll be back when you're ready for your round.'

'It was an interesting conference, I'd like to tell you about it.'

'If you have any notes on it, I'd like to see them some time,' she said, 'but not right now.'

Jane saw his face grow blank. 'Of course,' he said.

She left the room before they had to talk further.

It was hard. It was even harder because he seemed to have to come into the unit more often over the next three or four days, and each time she treated him in the same polite but distant way. She didn't like doing it. She got on with most people, she would have liked to be friends. But it was the only way she could cope. She just didn't want to start feeling again. Here she was starting a new life. And more heartache was no part of it.

Somehow she managed to keep him at a distance. She never saw him alone in her room. Their conversations were limited to purely medical matters. And slowly his manner grew distant, too. They merely were professional colleagues again.

This should have made her happy. No, she told herself, it *did* make her happy. It was what she wanted...or needed. But she hated it when she saw him change back into the abstracted man he had been before.

Forbidden fruits taste sweetest, she told herself. What had been between them had just been a physical thing, a hunger felt by their bodies. She could forget it. But it had been so long for her...

It was Friday afternoon, for once a quiet time. She had left Chris in her room, checking over some past case notes. As she walked into the corridor she saw Erica, white-faced, leaning against the wall.

'What's wrong, Erica?'

'Nothing. I just felt a bit sick and—'

'Erica! I'm your friend, remember. What's wrong?' Jane had already guessed. But this was worse than before.

'It's Martin. I think he's waiting for me outside.'

Erica was in quite a state, Jane noted, she was shaking with fear.

Erica went on, 'It'll be the end of the shift soon but I'm frightened to go out.'

Jane knew that there was far more violence in hospital now than there had been even when she had started training. Erica's fears could be well grounded. She said, 'I'll phone Security and see if—'

'What's the problem here?'

Jane hadn't heard Chris approach, didn't even know how much of the conversation he had heard. But he appeared to have heard enough. His face was black with rage. And his voice was icy cold.

Feeling rather nervous, Jane explained a little about the situation. 'Erica's having a little difficulty with her ex-partner. She's afraid that when she goes to the nurses' home he'll be waiting for her outside. I was just going to phone Security and—'

'No need to phone Security. I won't have any nurse who works for me scared to walk—'

'This is my ward, I'll look after my staff,' Jane snapped, which enraged Chris even more. 'I will deal with this if it's necessary,' he announced. 'All three of us will now go for a little walk in the sun, and don't argue.'

This was a new Chris to Jane. She had seen him cool but had never seen him angry. She didn't feel that she could cross him.

'All right,' she said. 'We'll go out in the sun for a minute.' She noted that even the terrified Erica seemed content to do what Chris said.

They went out into the sun, walked across the grass. 'Hey, wait!' an angry voice shouted from behind them. 'I want a word with you.'

'Keep walking and don't look round,' Chris said, and they did as he ordered.

There was the sound of feet on the grass behind them, and then suddenly Martin was in front of them, standing in their path. They either had to stop or walk round him. Chris decided to stop.

It was the first time Jane had ever seen Erica's ex-partner. Perhaps once he had been attractive, now his face was fattening. His hair was over-long and greasy, his clothes looked dirty. And he smelled of alcohol.

He pushed Jane to one side, grabbed Erica by the arm and said, 'I want a word with you.' Then he looked at Chris and Jane and added, 'And you two can get lost.'

'Take your hand off Erica,' Chris snarled. 'You're

assaulting her and you've already assaulted this lady. And I won't have it.'

'So you won't have it? Well, in that case you'd better— Aagh! Stop it, that hurts!'

Jane couldn't understand what was happening. Chris had reached out and appeared to be holding the man's shoulder just with one hand. But the man's face was now pasty white and he was obviously in great pain.

'Let go of Erica,' said Chris.

The man did so at once. Chris pulled him closer and whispered, 'If I see you in my hospital again, if I hear that you've been anywhere near any of my nurses, I'll see that you're really in trouble. Understand?' His voice rose. 'I said, do you understand?'

'Yes, I understand,' the man whimpered.

'Good. Now move, and move fast.'

Chris released Martin and he moved off, in a shambling trot. Once or twice he turned to look back at the group, but he never stopped moving.

'I think Erica should go to her room,' Chris said at last. 'The shift will soon be ended and she's a little upset. Of course, it is your decision, your responsibility to deal with your staff.'

'Of course. But I agree with you. Erica, you go and rest. I'll be with you later.'

'Right,' said Erica. 'Er…thank you, Mr Fielding.'

Chris said nothing, merely bowed his head. Erica walked towards the nurses' home.

'Security could have dealt with that,' Jane said. 'They're trained for that sort of thing. There was no reason for you to get involved.'

'Perhaps I wanted to get involved.'

'That was obvious. Incidentally, that man seemed to be in considerable pain. What did you do to him?'

'I pushed my fingers down the back of his clavicle. Remember your anatomy? There's a nerve centre there, very unpleasant if it's pressed.'

'A fine use of medical knowledge,' said Jane. 'Now I've got to go back to work.'

CHAPTER FIVE

AS SOON as she came off duty Jane went to see Erica to check that she was all right. She seemed to have made a quick and happy recovery. She thought that, with any luck, Martin would have been scared off. 'I've never see him look so frightened,' she said. 'Your Chris really terrified him.'

'He's not my Chris. And I'm not sure I approve of what he did. We could have talked about things in a civilised manner.'

'Martin isn't civilised and when he's drunk there's no talking to him.'

Jane didn't say anything because she really agreed with Erica. Instead, she said, 'Doctors are supposed to stop pain, not cause it.'

Erica giggled. 'Well, I liked what he did. It was good to see Martin suffer for a change instead of me. And I thought Chris looked wonderful when he got mad. Didn't you think he looked wonderful?'

'No. I don't like big, tough, macho men who resort to violence.'

Erica giggled again. 'Don't tell him that, will you?'

'I think I already have. Why shouldn't I tell him what I think?'

''Cos you'll disappoint him. He did it largely to impress you.'

'Don't be silly! He was acting out of concern for a nurse—you—and you have him to thank for it. It wasn't for me. No one likes being the object of a…a brawl.'

'Of course not,' said Erica. 'He lost his temper. I just wonder why.'

When she went back to her room Jane thought about what Erica had said and rather gloomily felt that there was some element of truth in it. A primitive, elemental part of her had responded to the sight of an enraged man…defending her? This was ridiculous. She was a nurse, he was a doctor, both were dedicated to alleviating pain, not causing it. And why had he been so angry? She found out the next day. But first there was her work.

Like many parents, Lily Parr was horrified when she first saw her baby in her incubator.

The baby hadn't been due for another six weeks but she had tripped and fallen at home. When she'd started to bleed her husband had phoned for an ambulance, the summoned obstetrician had examined her and decided he would deliver at once by caesarean section. So far things were going quite well.

Lily, of course, had been recovering in bed, but she'd worried so much about her baby that eventually she'd been placed in a wheelchair and brought along to see her.

'She looks tiny,' she whispered to Jane. 'And all those tubes and things and that machinery. What are they all for?'

'They're to help your baby through the first few weeks of life,' Jane said. 'When you're feeling a bit stronger I'll tell you about them all.'

'My baby… Can I hold her? Or can I reach in through one of those holes and touch her?'

Jane sighed. She understood the great need a mother had to hold her baby, to bond with her. But at baby Parr's stage of development, it wasn't a good idea.

'Perhaps you'd better not touch her for a day or two. But what you can do is get very close to the incubator. Then put your hands, one above her head, one above her feet, about three inches away from her. Then gently move your hands towards each other and away again, but not ever touching your baby.'

'Not touching? What good will that do?'

'Surprisingly, quite a lot. The baby can feel you near her, loving her. If you talk to her she'll hear you. She's been listening to you for a long time now and she knows your voice.'

'And even not touching her works?'

'Oh, yes, it works,' said Jane. 'I know it sounds a bit fanciful, but I know it works. Your baby will feel you.'

'All right, I'll try. But I had hoped to…to hold her.' Lily was having difficulty holding back her tears.

Jane squeezed her shoulder. 'Just try what I've suggested. See what it's like and don't forget the talking.'

So Lily did as she was told. Jane watched for a minute, saw that Lily knew what to do and left. And when she returned fifteen minutes later she saw that Lily had that rapt expression that meant she had made contact with her baby even though she hadn't touched her. She looked up at Jane. 'She can hear me,' she said wonderingly. 'She knows I'm here.'

'Of course she knows you're here,' said Jane.

*   *   *

It had been a good shift. Jane had been engrossed, had enjoyed herself. It was always good to see a mother and baby thriving and know that it was partly through your efforts.

As she walked away from the unit, through the hospital parklands, she realised that she felt happy. It was as if a great shadow was falling from her. She was getting to like this place, feeling at home with her colleagues, getting on top of the work.

And her work on the unit was beginning to take effect. The staff were happier, their grumbling at the new shift system was largely good-humoured. It was early days yet, but she thought she was going to be successful.

This life was different from that in London. The past was receding into her memory.

Almost unconsciously she felt for her wedding ring and twisted it. Then she realised something else. This was a nervous trick that she had almost forgotten. Once she would have felt for solace in the ring a dozen times a day. Now she hardly ever touched it.

She was walking along the side of a road that ran through the hospital grounds when she heard the sound of a car engine behind her. She stepped onto the grass. The car passed her, a large burgundy Range Rover. Where had she seen…? Chris's car! The vehicle stopped, the passenger door opened and a voice growled, 'Get in.'

She peered inside, to see a distinctly angry-looking Chris frowning at her.

'What do you—'

'Just get in. I'll answer all your questions later.'

Her first reaction was to slam the door and walk off

across the grass. But then she realised that she didn't really want to walk off. 'Just get in the car?' she asked. 'With you? What for?'

'You'll never find out if you don't get in, will you?'

'You're not very polite. You could at least say please.'

He sighed. 'Please, get in the car, Jane. We're going to talk and I've got a better place in mind than the unit or anywhere at the hospital. Don't want a scene, do we?'

No, she didn't want a scene. So she climbed in the car, shut the door and clicked on her seat belt. 'If you were really keen on talking to me you would have come round and opened the door for me,' she said.

'And you would have run off and I'd have chased you and what a sight that would have been for all concerned. Now, before anything else, how's Erica?'

'She's a lot better, thanks, feeling quite cheerful. She's very grateful to you. She thinks better of your actions than I do.' Jane paused then added, 'But I guess that if it had been me having trouble, I'd agree with her.'

'That's honest of you. But, then, I think you always are honest. Sometimes it's not a good idea.'

She didn't want to think about that. 'Where are we going and why?' she asked.

'For a while we're just driving. You haven't got any plans for the next hour or two, have you?'

'No, but—'

'Just enjoy the drive. You've had a hard day and it's going to be a glorious evening.'

That was true. They drove out of town and headed up a small road that wound high into the Wolds. Jane hadn't yet explored this bit of her new surroundings and she was pleasantly pleased with the greenness of the steep hills, the white chalk showing through.

He drove for about an hour then turned onto a track through woodland and eventually parked on a patch where they could see down into the valley below and the misty edges of moor beyond that. 'The Vale of York,' he said. 'I come here just to sit and look. I come when I have the chance and when I need peace for a while.'

'So how often is that?'

'Too often,' he said. 'There's a tree trunk we can sit on along there. Shall we sit in the open air?'

So they did. Chris said nothing for a while and Jane was quite content to sit there calmly with him. It was an entrancing spot he had picked, and she thought she might come here herself. Would it be the same without him?

'I wanted to get well away from the hospital,' he said eventually. 'For a while I wanted to forget that you are the ward manager and I am a doctor, and there is a unit to run that we largely do together. I want to think about us with you just as a woman and me just as a man.'

'That's not easy to do. And I'm not sure that it's a good idea anyway. We are both carrying a fair amount of…emotional baggage that gets in our way.'

'True. But why are you ignoring me? You walk out of the room when I walk in. You don't smile at me when I smile at you. You're treating me as some kind of social leper. What's more, people are beginning to notice. My SHO asked me yesterday what I'd done to offend you.'

'That's all I need,' she said tightly. 'Yes, that's all I need. I'm trying to do a difficult job in a professional manner and what I get is gossip. Chris, I am not ignoring you. I'm being purely professional. Not one of our charges has suffered because of…of what happened between us. I think you're a wonderful doctor and I'm happy to work with you.'

'Being purely professional,' he said, his voice now much softer. 'Is that all we have in common?'

She shuddered as she thought of that night, of how much more they had in common. But she had to be strong. 'After we…well, after, I think it better for everyone if we keep apart. And, after all, apparently you are still a married man.'

'Only just. It won't last much longer, our lawyers are working on things right now.'

'Well, I still don't want any long-term relationship. Anyway, Chris, I've told you my story. Tell me yours. Why did you part from your wife? I think I'm entitled to know.'

He was silent for so long that she began to worry. Had she upset him that much? Still, it was a fair question. Then he said, 'Yes, you are entitled to know. But I promised her that I would never discuss our affairs with anyone. And even for you, I won't break that promise. All I can say is that…I feel that I did nothing wrong. And I know that she would agree with me.'

Jane thought about this for a minute then looked at Chris's anxious face. 'OK, I can understand that,' she said. 'Though I am curious. But I like a man who can keep a secret. Still…I like you, Chris, I like your company. But being with you, talking to you, enjoying being with you, it's a pleasure I just can't have.'

'Why not? Why this coldness? Can't we at least be friends? It would mean so much to me, Jane.'

She had to tell the truth. 'It's not coldness. Well, it is, but it's something I put on to protect myself.'

'Protect yourself? From me?'

She wished he hadn't forced her to say it, but she might as well tell him the truth. 'No, from myself.'

She had admitted it now, both to him and to herself. She was attracted to him. But she didn't want to think or talk more about it. She wondered if she could move onto a safer subject. 'Anyway,' she went on, 'why concentrate on me? You're young, attractive, apparently available, you must have lots of offers of...of female companionship. Why not pick someone else?'

'Possibly I do have women interested in me,' he said vaguely, 'but if I do I'm not interested in them. Fiona drops in to see me quite often...if I'm honest, more often than I really want her to. But the difference between you and her is...' His voice trailed away and she could tell he was thinking. 'Has Fiona talked to you about me?' he asked, deceptively calmly.

'She seems very fond of you,' Jane said, going slightly red.

'I see. So you have discussed me.'

It was time to be brutally honest. 'I thought her work on the unit might be affected. And she's a good nurse, I need people like her. We have to work together, for the good of our patients. So I told her that I was not in any way interested in you except professionally.'

'And has her work improved since then?' Still that deceptively calm voice.

In fact, he was right. There definitely was a better

atmosphere. Cautiously, she said, 'We're all pulling together as a team now. I think I'm getting everyone's confidence. But this has probably got nothing to do with you.'

'Possibly not. But I still think I'd better have a word with her myself.'

'No, don't! I have—we both have—to work with her. Like I said, she's a good nurse.'

'A quiet life is all very well but some prices are too high to pay.' For a moment he seemed to think and then he said, 'But we'll change the subject for now. How would you like to come to a party with me next week?'

'A party! The last thing we need is to be seen partying together.'

'You might enjoy it,' he said imperturbably. 'Little sandwiches, orange juice jellies and various games.'

'Jellies? Games?'

'Both very necessary. This is James's birthday party, he likes games. Most of his play group is coming and he's very much looking forward to it. He asked if you could come, he thinks you're a great story-teller. Will you come?'

She suspected she was fooling herself. Certainly this appeared to be nothing more than an invitation to a child's birthday party. But it would mean she would be together with Chris. And she didn't know where that might lead. The sensible thing would be to refuse the invitation. But... 'All right. I'd love to come,' she said. Then she thought for a few moments more and added, 'And don't have a word with Fiona. I will.'

Lucy Granger had been born prematurely and weighed only three pounds two ounces. She was instantly admitted to SCBU and had the usual dedicated medical care.

And it looked as if Lucy would pull through. She had survived a week and was apparently thriving. Her parents called every day, but no longer had that frightened look that Jane knew so well. Now they were allowing themselves to hope. And so was Jane.

But the baby was still very small. 'Lucy's doing well so far,' she told the parents, 'but she's got a long way to go before she's completely out of danger. Still...we're all very happy with her progress.'

It was early afternoon, Jane had finished what she wanted to do on the wards and was now looking gloomily at next year's requisitions forms. How could she possibly guess what supplies she might need in eighteen months' time?

There was a knock on her door and Matt peeped round. He was on his own. Chris was somewhere meeting hospital managers, fighting for extra money to order the new apnoea monitors he had seen at York.

'If you've got a minute,' Matt said, 'I'd appreciate a bit of advice. There's something I don't like about Lucy Granger.'

It was one of the things Jane liked about the man. He was willing to learn from anyone. Having been a nurse himself, he knew that nurses who had worked in one discipline for years often knew far more than a new young doctor. 'She seemed all right this morning,' she said. 'A bit grizzly perhaps, but that was all.'

However, she knew that things could change in a matter of minutes.

'You know she had a patent ductus arteriosus?'

'Yes, I knew. But I thought it was closing. Chris said to keep an eye on it but there was no need to worry. It was closing.'

'Well, I think it's opened. She's starting to look a bit jaundiced and I'm not happy about her heartbeat.'

'Ah,' said Jane. She stood, dropped her pen and said, 'I'll have a quick scrub and see you there in a couple of minutes. Should we try to get in touch with Chris?'

'I've tried. Apparently he's switched his bleeper off. This looks like my decision.'

'Our decision,' Jane said.

As she scrubbed her hands she quickly thought over what she knew about patent ductus arteriosus—usually referred to as PDA. The ductus arteriosus was a passageway in unborn children linking two blood vessels leaving the heart. In most children it closed at birth, but in one in five premature babies it remained open— or patent—for a while. The condition wasn't hard to detect, and usually just reducing the amount of fluid in the body was enough to deal with the matter. Lucy had been treated this way, but it sounded as if the condition had got worse.

Matt was waiting by Lucy's incubator. Jane had a quick look at the notes. Blood pressure up. Then she leaned over to look at the baby. She was more yellow than she had been that morning and her breathing seemed to be troubled.

'Try the external pulses,' Matt said.

Gently, Jane felt Lucy's foot, her groin, the top of her head. The pulse was there, far too strong. Matt handed her his stethoscope. She listened to Lucy's chest and heard the continuous murmur that suggested blood was not following its proper route.

'I would say that is PDA,' she said, 'and my opinion is that surgery is indicated. Let's give her a Doppler ultrasound scan to be absolutely sure and then get the paediatric surgeon down here to look at her.'

'Without asking Chris?'

'Try and get in touch with him again and keep trying. But carry on anyway.'

Matt looked undecided a moment. Then he grinned. 'I can make a fool of myself,' he said. 'This might not need surgery at all. But if there's even a small chance that we're right, then we've got to get started. I'll bleep the surgeon.'

They were in luck, the surgeon was available and down to the ward in minutes. He agreed with their decision and ordered Lucy up to the Theatre as soon as possible.

'We have to get in touch with the parents,' Jane said. 'We need consent.'

Matt winced. 'It's always been Chris who has asked for that,' he said. 'He likes to explain things to them, make sure they know what they're signing.'

Jane lifted her phone and dialled the postnatal ward number. They were in luck. Lucy's father was in the ward, talking to Lucy's mother. 'Get over there,' she said to Matt. 'Chris says that talking to parents is one of the hardest parts of the job. You'd better get some practice in.'

'Well, keep phoning him for me.'

Eventually it was Jane who managed to contact Chris. In common with all the others in the meeting, he had been asked to turn off his bleeper. When he came out of the meeting he turned it on again—and found an urgent message from Jane.

As always, he listened calmly to what she had to say and then asked to speak to Matt, who had just returned with the consent form signed. The conversation was short.

'He agrees with what we've done,' said Matt. 'He's coming down. Says he would have been angry if we'd acted any differently.'

'If you'd acted differently,' Jane said. 'You took the decision.'

'Yes,' said Matt. 'I suppose I did.'

Some hours later Lucy was returned to the ward. The operation had been a success. Lucy should now do well. Jane talked to the anxious parents, managed to calm them. After that she decided she was entitled to a rest. She made herself a pot of strong sweet coffee, sat in her room with her eyes closed and drank.

After ten minutes she felt stronger, energised as the caffeine and the sugar hit her bloodstream. There were things to do and, compared with keeping alive tiny Lucy Granger, they were easy.

She hadn't seen Fiona for a while but knew she had been working in the low-dependency room. In five minutes she'd be coming down to the nurses' room for a coffee herself. When there was the sound of her laugh outside, and the rattle of her feet in the corridor, Jane opened her door and called her. 'Fiona. Have you a minute, please?'

Fiona came in and sat down. As ever, she looked pleased with herself. 'Not a problem, is there?' she asked. 'Things are quiet in our room. But I gather you've been having fun with a PDA.'

'I wouldn't say fun is the word,' Jane said, 'but I think we saved the baby's life. No, I'm afraid this isn't a professional matter. Just a quick chat. It's personal and I hope we can deal with it in a civilised manner.'

'Personal?' Fiona said. 'I thought we had our personal relationship worked out.' Her voice was cool, her eyes wary.

'I may have misled you in our recent conversation about Mr Fielding—Chris. I think what we said bound me to an agreement I might not want to keep. My life is my own, Fiona. I shall enter into whatever relationships I wish.' Jane hoped she sounded more confident than she felt.

Fiona bowed her head for a moment. Then she looked up, smiled and said, 'You've slept with him, haven't you?'

The question was so unexpected that Jane couldn't stop the flush of guilt that flooded her face. She looked at Fiona, speechless.

Still smiling, Fiona nodded, as if they were two old friends sharing a happy secret. 'He's good, isn't he?' she asked carelessly. 'He knows how to make a woman feel that she's the centre of his life, the one thing that matters to him. I think he does it to everyone.'

Jane's voice cracked. 'You mean he's…you and he have…'

'Well, his wife has gone,' Fiona pointed out reasonably, 'so he makes do with me. He's still in love with her, you know. And at the moment I'm the closest thing.'

'You've slept with him?'

'Only a couple of times. In that bedroom with the light on the dressing-table and the dark blue sheets. It's quite something to wake with his arms round you, isn't it? I'm sure you know. Well, I said it to you once before, at the interview. May the best woman win.' Fiona stood and walked out.

Jane's head was whirling. Chris couldn't have slept with Fiona…and yet the story was so convincing. This was all too much. The exhilaration she had felt not ten minutes before had now evaporated.

Life had been much more serene without men or relationships. Now it seemed she was being dragged into more problems, more heartache. The simplest thing would be to forget Chris, to get on with her simple life. But she knew she couldn't do that. She just had to know the truth.

The rest of the day passed somehow. Jane was vaguely aware of decisions she took, work she performed. Fortunately, nothing much of importance happened. As soon as she got to her room that night she phoned Chris. She had learned on the unit that he was at home.

'Chris, this is Jane.' She knew her voice sounded nervous.

On the other hand, his voice was cheerful and confident. 'Jane! Good to hear from you. How are you?'

She couldn't think what to say next. All day she had been determined that she would phone him as soon as she could. What she hadn't done was decide what to say. She sat there speechless, the phone clutched to her.

After a while he spoke again, his voice this time slightly concerned. 'Jane, are you there? Is everything all right?'

So she just asked. 'Chris, did you sleep with Fiona?'

She hadn't thought about what answer she might get. But she certainly wasn't expecting what did happen. He laughed. A real laugh, he thought something was funny. And she didn't think it was funny at all. 'You've been talking to her,' he said. 'Did she tell you that?'

'Yes, she did. And she was pretty convincing. Chris, I can do without all this. I want a quiet life, I want to be at peace.'

'Don't we all? Right, Jane, I think we've been pussy-footing around each other long enough. We need to get a few things straight. We need a proper talk and I'll tell you about sleeping with Fiona. I'd like you to come to supper with me tonight at the Escott Arms. They do good suppers and I'll take a taxi so I can have a drink.'

'The Escott Arms! That's practically an annexe of the hospital. We'll be seen there, gossiped about. Tomorrow everyone will be talking about it.'

'Perhaps that's what I want. People to see me having a good time.'

She couldn't help herself, she giggled. 'Mr Fielding, if people see you having a good time, they'll wonder. You'll disappoint them. You'll not be living up to your reputation as an old misery.'

'That would be terrible. But I'll risk it. Shall I pick you up at about nine?'

She was not going to have that. The entire nurses' home would be ringing with gossip minutes after he arrived. 'No, I'll meet you at the Escott Arms.'

'Well, may I walk you home afterwards? Perhaps have a cup of coffee in your room?'

'That's going too far on a first date,' she said. 'But perhaps you can walk me to the door. So, Escott Arms at nine. I'll be there.' She rang off.

She walked across the corridor, knocked at Erica's door. 'I'm going to the Escott Arms for supper with Chris Fielding,' she said. 'What shall I wear?'

'Something special,' Erica said, 'something really, really special.'

He was waiting for her at a table in the front of the hotel so she didn't need to walk in on her own. After much hesitation and a consideration of both their wardrobes, she and Erica had decided that a pink dress would be best. It showed her arms, rather a lot of chest, set off her blonde hair. In case it got cold—or perhaps just in case—she wore a dark blue shawl round her shoulders.

He stood, and his eyes widened in admiration as she walked up to him. 'You do look beautiful,' he said.

'Thank you, kind sir. And you look quite good yourself.' He was wearing light-coloured trousers and T-shirt, a blue blazer in some lightweight material. She had noticed that whatever he wore he looked well.

It was still very warm. He led her through the building, to the back where there was an alcove, in the open air but shaded from the sun. 'This place has a good name for supper dishes,' he said. 'I recommend the seafood omelette, we could have a bottle of white wine with it.'

'Sounds good. Whatever you recommend.'

A waiter was hovering nearby, Chris gave the order and then they were on their own. 'So this meeting with me in public is some kind of a declaration, is it?' she asked.

'I think it is. I'm showing that I've got a life to lead. Is your agreeing to meet me here also a declaration? And, if so, what are you declaring?'

'I suppose it is a declaration. But I'm not yet sure what I'm doing here. Partly it's to do with Fiona. I'm not going to have my life ruled by someone else's prejudices.'

'And I thought it was the pleasure of my company.'

'Well, perhaps a bit of that, too,' she said.

Their wine was served next. She sipped it and it was marvellous.

'We have important talking to do,' he said, 'but we'll wait till we've eaten. Everything looks better and easier when you have a full stomach.'

'How did you know I was starving?' she asked.

So they chatted amiably about the plans for the hospital and nothing much else exciting. Their omelettes came, with a salad and hot rolls, and were as wonderful as he had said. And afterwards they had home-made ice cream. Then the dishes were cleared away. They sat with another glass of white wine each and he said. 'Yes, I did sleep with Fiona.'

She stared at him, her jaw dropped. What had he just said? 'You...you slept with Fiona?'

'I certainly did. I woke up and there she was by my side, her hair spread across the pillow.'

'I hope she'd had it freshly dyed,' croaked Jane. 'No dark roots showing.'

He grinned. 'I'm afraid I didn't notice, I was too busy panicking.' He picked up his glass, sipped a little and then said, 'I suppose I'd better tell you the full story before you throw some of this excellent wine over me.'

Jane drank from her own glass. 'I suppose you'd better.'

'It was on one of those few occasions when Mrs Mansell couldn't manage to stay over. There was an emergency, I had to stay late on the unit. Fiona offered to come and babysit and stay the night. I got in very late, absolutely done in. The house was quiet, I went straight to bed and was asleep within seconds.'

'And?'

'I woke up to find a woman in bed with me. It was Fiona, naked like me. It was quite a shock. She'd crept into bed while I was asleep.'

Jane thought about this. 'And were your arms round her?'

'Very possibly. But it certainly wasn't intentional.'

'So what happened next?'

'Sorry to let down my reputation as a great lover, but nothing happened. I was embarrassed. In order, she was coy, brazen and then angry.'

'You turned her down?'

'Of course I turned her down! I tried to be pleasant about it but no way was I going to have sex with Fiona so that she could feel better about things. Perhaps I should have lost my temper with her, but I didn't.'

'And then?'

He shrugged. 'I felt sorry for her. And perhaps because of that I said something a bit stupid. I said I did like her, and who knows what the situation might be like in a few months? She evidently took this as a promise that all she had to do was wait a while.'

'I see,' said Jane. 'You know, she didn't exactly lie to me. She just let me draw my own conclusions. Come on, finish the story off.'

'Not much more to tell. I faced the other way while she climbed out of bed, she got dressed downstairs and she didn't stay for breakfast. You do believe me, don't you, Jane?'

'Oh, yes, I believe you. Now, can we talk about something else?' She was amazed to discover how relieved she felt. Of course, she hadn't really believed Fiona's story. But still…she felt better now she'd heard about it from Chris.

As she had said, the Escott Arms was almost an annexe of the hospital. There were quite a few staff there who she recognised, and Chris recognised even more. They said hello to several couples and Jane saw several people giving them knowing looks. No secrets here.

'We're certainly going to be talked about,' he said, 'but that's what I wanted. What about you?'

'I don't know. I came here intending to lead a quiet life, to work and do very little else. Now things are happening, I don't know if I can cope.' It was now dusk. She pulled her shawl round her shoulders and said, 'Can we go now? I have to think and I find that walking helps me think.'

'Of course we can go,' he said. They walked through the hotel and into the hospital grounds. It was pleasant walking on the grass, smelling the scents of midsummer. It was almost dark now, she didn't object when he took her hand.

'We have to start with the most important fact of my life so far,' she said. 'My husband John. I loved him and we got married. He was taken ill and he died. He took about three years to die, and after about a year we knew what was going to happen. We both knew, Chris, and after a while we managed to talk about it. It's hard to cope with that kind of thing, you're not entitled to feel sorry for yourself because you're not the one who is dying.'

'You're entitled to feel sorry for yourself,' he said quietly. 'Perhaps you had the harder part to play.'

'Perhaps. Anyway, one way you learn to cope is you shut off all emotion. I loved him still...but I had a job to do, a life to lead. I didn't shut him out, I looked after him and loved him, but I pushed my personal feelings to the back. So...now...I just don't know if I want to feel again. It hurts. With you...when we made love it was wonderful. But it was just physical. I'm not objecting. Like I said, it was wonderful. But it was just bodies and I've got to keep it that way.' She paused a moment and then said, 'You know what I mean when I say it was just physical, don't you? And you're not mad at me?'

'I'm not mad at you, I couldn't be. But I can't agree with you. What we had was more than physical and you know it. Now, in some way, the two of us are...locked together.'

'But I don't want that! I couldn't stand the pain again!'

He stopped, wrapped his arms round her and held

her gently. She could just see the gleaming of his eyes in the near darkness. 'The last thing I want to do is cause you pain,' he said. 'I told you that before.'

She could feel the tears sliding down her cheeks. Why did she have to give way, to feel so weak when she was with him?

'You're crying,' he said. 'I wish you wouldn't.'

'I just can't help it. And I'm surprised, because I thought I was all cried out. But I'm not really miserable, I think I'm afraid.'

He bent his head, touched his lips to her cheeks and wiped away the tears. 'I think we have a future,' he whispered to her. 'I don't know what it is but I know it's there. I won't hurry you, I won't make demands on you, but I want you to know that you...mean a lot to me.'

He was silent for a moment and then she realised he was laughing. 'That must count as one of the great romantic declarations,' he said. 'You mean a lot to me.'

'For now, that's plenty. It's all I want. And it makes things easier for me, too, because I can say it back. I think you mean a lot to me, Chris. Now, will you take me home?'

'Do I get a farewell kiss?'

'Only on the doorstep,' she said.

Of course, Jane knew that the news would get out. They had been seen by too many people. On Monday morning she was greeted with grins and asked if she'd enjoyed her meal at the Escott Arms.

'Superb food,' she said airily, 'and the company was

good as well.' If people wanted to gossip she might as well give them something to gossip about.

Unfortunately, Fiona was on the same shift as her. Jane would have preferred it if they hadn't had to meet for a while. But Fiona was there, and Fiona was not at all happy about Jane going out with Chris. It showed in her work. She deliberately caused trouble, slacked off and was insolent in all her remarks.

Jane waited a few days. She didn't want a confrontation but she was not going to avoid one. And eventually the time came. Jane had told Fiona to supervise Sue, the student nurse who was learning about working with neonates. Sue was to feed a baby, Fiona to watch and advise. When Jane looked into the little ward, there was the student doing the best she could but obviously terrified. There was no sign of Fiona.

'Fiona told me to get on with it,' Sue said hesitantly. 'She's gone for a cup of coffee.'

'Well, you're not doing badly,' Jane said, 'but hold the baby like this...and she'll feed easier.'

She stayed with Sue and watched as the baby was laid in its incubator, and then put her head round the door of the nurses' room. 'Fiona. My room. Now!'

Fiona came to her room, taking just long enough to be insolent again. She didn't knock, moved straight to a chair.

'Stand up! When I want you to sit down I'll tell you.'

Fiona looked at Jane, shocked. 'But I—'

'You're late! When I say now, I mean it. If this had been an emergency there would have been trouble.'

'But there isn't an emergency and I'm entitled to—'

'You're entitled to nothing. Your behaviour over the past week has been appalling. I've had occasion to speak to you three times, minor faults certainly but minor faults can lead to major problems. That student nurse should never have been left on her own! This is your last verbal warning. The next one will be a written warning and will possibly lead to disciplinary action. Do I make myself clear?'

Fiona was now white-faced, unable to speak. She licked her dry lips and then her temper overcame her common sense. 'This isn't about nursing, is it? This is about Chris. Everyone knows you've been seeing him, you're trying to go behind my back and—'

'Nurse Law! I don't choose to discuss my private life with you and I'm not interested in your private life. Our relationship is purely professional. Now, buck your ideas up or I'll have you out. Is that clear?'

Fiona stared at her, wide-eyed.

'I *said* is that clear?' Jane repeated, softly this time, and Fiona realised she'd have to reply.

'It's clear,' she said.

'Good. Then get out and do your job.'

Fiona left. Jane managed to keep her face stern until the door closed, then started shaking with reaction. She hadn't enjoyed disciplining Fiona, but she'd known she had to do something. And she had seen more than fear in Fiona's eyes. There was malice there still. She wondered if it was something she ought to worry about, then decided not to.

There was something else. Before she'd come to this job she would not have dreamed of talking to someone as she had talked to Fiona. The job was changing her. Or was she changing herself?

CHAPTER SIX

THE party was at three on Saturday. Jane had never been to a children's party before, well, never one for healthy children. There had been parties on the ward when she'd been a children's nurse dealing with older children. Some had been occasions of joy. Others had been heart-breaking. This party was going to be different, for a variety of reasons.

She phoned Chris on Saturday morning, just wanting to have an excuse. 'The party this afternoon. Would you like me to come early to help?'

Even though she'd talked to him the day before, she still got a thrill when hearing his voice. 'That would be great. Mrs Mansell is coming but I'm sure you could help her. To tell the truth, I'm a bit scared. I've never run a kids' party in my own home. Having you there will give me confidence.'

'As if you needed confidence! How's James?'

'He's excited already. Got all his birthday cards lined up neatly.'

'Tell him I'm looking forward to seeing him.'

Erica came into her room as Jane got dressed that afternoon. She wasn't sure quite what to wear—a party outfit or something workmanlike. In the end she put on dark trousers and a coloured shirt that would be easy to wash. She found an apron with animals on it, which she'd worn on the children's ward, and wrapped it round her waist with a flourish.

'You're like a girl on her first date,' Erica said, smiling. 'You've got that excited look. This is good for you.'

'This isn't a date. It's going to be hard work.' Jane noticed that although Erica had smiled, there had been a touch of sadness in her voice. She decided not to comment on it.

'It'll be good for that man as well,' Erica went on. 'I think he's already got a bit less stiff, he's easing off. When his wife left him, we all felt so sorry for him. He was still a good, conscientious doctor and when it was needed he could talk well to the parents, as kind as anything. But other than that there were no smiles, no social graces, never dropped in for a coffee and a chat. You know, the little things that make life fun. But he's changing now. And it's you that's done it.'

'That's not because of me. It's because time is passing.'

'Of course,' Erica said.

Jane called at a shop on the way to Chris's house and bought James a Thomas the Tank Engine model that he didn't already possess. She also bought some Thomas pyjamas, a book and a card. Then, for a laugh, she bought Chris a present. A miniature bottle of Malt whisky. She had them all wrapped and then set off to drive to the party.

She was not sure how she felt. This was another step forward with Chris. But where was it leading?

When she arrived Mrs Mansell let her in. 'They're getting bathed and changed upstairs,' Mrs Mansell announced. 'They'll be down in a minute. Come into the kitchen. You'll be wanting a mug of tea.' This last was a statement, not an invitation.

Jane followed her into the kitchen and was poured a mug of tea. Then she said, 'What can I do first? I've brought my apron.'

This met with Mrs Mansell's approval. 'Goody bags,' she said. 'There's a list of children's names here, you can write them on the goody bags and then fill them with these little bits of things.'

So Jane put on her apron and did as she was instructed, while drinking her mug of tea. Mrs Mansell was baking cakes of some sort, a wonderful smell filled the kitchen. To one side was a cake in the form of an engine, with three candles as chimneys. Jane thought it was brilliant.

The two women worked steadily together. When the goody bags were filled they went to clear the dining-room table, spread it with a cloth and paper napkins on top. Then there were sandwiches, jellies, cakes, all the exciting things that children loved. 'How good are you at blowing up balloons?' Mrs Mansell asked. 'There's a couple of packets there. Children love balloons.' So Jane blew up balloons and fixed them round the room.

There was the rattle of feet on the stairs, the door burst open and in rushed James. 'Hello, Jane,' he shouted. 'This is my party.'

'Don't you look smart?' Jane said. 'In your new waistcoat and your bow-tie. I'll bet you'll be the smartest boy at your party.'

'I bought them for him,' said Mrs Mansell with a doting smile.

Then Chris came into the room, and Jane felt the

usual little lurch of her heart. It happened every time she saw him now, no matter how short a time since she'd last seen him. He was dressed in a similar outfit to her own, dark trousers and a coloured shirt. He looked approvingly at her apron. 'I see you've come to work,' he said.

'Just helping Mrs Mansell. She's got it all organised.' She turned to James. 'Now, birthday boy, these are for you.'

The card was placed on the sideboard with the others and soon afterwards the torn wrapping paper was on the floor. Jane had got it right. James had neither the engine nor the book and was delighted with both.

'This is silly but I got you a present, too,' Jane whispered to Chris when they had a moment to themselves. She handed over the little packet. 'Don't open it yet, it's only a little thing.'

'A present from you could never be a little thing. I shall—'

The doorbell rang. 'Here we go,' said Jane. 'That sounds like the first of your guests.'

He put the little box in his pocket. 'Party time,' he muttered.

There were ten guests altogether—that was ten children and ten mothers. Jane was rather amused by the reaction to her from the mothers. Chris introduced her as 'Jane—a friend of mine'. The mothers were obviously curious as to how far the friendship went.

'We've not seen you here before,' Arabella, definitely pushy, said. 'Have you known Chris long?'

'We work together. Chris told me about this party and I offered to help out.'

'I see,' said Arabella. 'So shall we be seeing even more of you?'

Jane smiled her sweetest smile. 'Who can tell?' she asked.

Five of the mothers stayed and were firmly conducted to the kitchen by Mrs Mansell. 'I've made you a pot of tea,' she told them. 'We'll send for you if we need you.' Then the party started.

It was a good party as such parties went. Jane was a bit surprised to see Chris happily and efficiently organising the games, he was not going to let anyone else take over his work as a father. That impressed her. It impressed her more when she saw that he was enjoying it. Chris was a natural father. She had sadly seen too many families in which this was not the case. There was the usual number of tears and squabbles, especially with pass the parcel and musical chairs.

Polly Waites, the loudest and apparently most confident child, fell over and hurt her head, and only Jane could pick her up and comfort her and persuade her that little Jenny had not done it on purpose. After kissing Jane and hugging her with sticky fingers, Polly was quietened.

The meal passed without too many spillages and James blew his candles out with one puff. Soon afterwards it was time to go.

'I was watching you,' Arabella said. 'You're good with kids, aren't you? I do hope we'll be seeing you a lot with Chris and James.' She looked pointedly at the wedding ring on Jane's finger.

'I work with Chris,' said Jane. 'It's Saturday, I'm not on call, I was just helping him out.'

Twenty minutes later, everyone was gone. Mrs

Mansell offered to stay but Chris said she had done a wonderful job, but he would clear up himself.'

'Well, I'm sure you'll be all right since you've got a bit of help,' Mrs Mansell said, looking pointedly at Jane. And she went.

'She likes you,' said Chris, as the taxi picked up Mrs Mansell's sturdy form.

'You've got a real treasure there,' said Jane, 'but you did the really hard work, organising the games.'

'I'd sooner do a dozen ward rounds than that again. Why does ten times as many children make a hundred times as much trouble?'

'That's life,' said Jane.

Somehow, it was understood that she wouldn't leave at once. She and Chris walked back into the house and discovered James sitting impatiently in front of the television. 'I want to watch my new video,' he said. 'Daddy, would you like to watch?'

'Don't argue, watch with him,' Jane whispered to Chris. 'I'll start on the clearing up.'

'But you shouldn't—'

'I said don't argue. Sitting with you will make him happy. It's his birthday. And I'm fine.'

So Jane cleared away, washed, tidied and stored left-over cakes in an assortment of tins that Mrs Mansell had conveniently left handy. When the first video ended Chris took James upstairs, bathed him again and put on his pyjamas. By now Jane had finished and the three of them sat and watched the second video.

James was lying in his father's lap, and every couple of minutes Chris would stroke his son's hair. Jane thought that father and son made a lovely picture. Then she wondered about Chris's ex-wife. The woman must have been mad! Who could leave a man like this?

James fell asleep in his father's arms. Chris carried him up to bed. When he returned he took the small parcel from the mantelpiece. 'Now it's my turn. I'm going to open my present now,' he said. He came to sit by her on the couch and then tore away the red paper. 'Laphroaigh! How did you know that was my favourite?'

'Just a guess. I'm glad you like it.'

'We'll both have a drop later. Now I want to buy you a present. And a card. When's your birthday? Is it soon?'

'It is soon.' Her voice was low when she replied. 'Tenth of July. But I don't celebrate it. Not now.'

He picked up on her distress. 'Want to tell me why?' he asked quietly.

'Last year my husband died on the ninth of July. The day before my birthday.'

'Ah. I see.'

She was glad he didn't say anything more, there was nothing helpful that he could possibly have said. Instead he put his arm round her shoulders in a comforting, non-sexual way.

After a while she said, 'It doesn't matter, you know. I'm getting over it.'

'It does matter. And pain does take time—no matter how prepared you are, no matter how intelligent, sensible you are about things. You can say that it was for the best, it was bound to happen, think of the future. But the hurt is still there.'

'You know,' she said. 'I can tell you know. You've suffered yourself.'

'Everyone suffers at some time.'

They sat there together on the couch and she realised she was tired. She laid her head on his shoulder, slumped towards him. Just before she closed her eyes she realised that this was a thing she never did. But she was doing it now.

She woke, perhaps ten minutes, perhaps an hour later. She glanced at the face so close to her own. Chris's eyes were closed and by the rhythmic rise and fall of his chest she could tell that he was sleeping, too. She tried to move without disturbing him, but instantly his eyes flashed open. There was the momentary doubt—just where was he, what was happening?—and then he recollected. He smiled at her, leaned over to kiss her on the forehead.

'We both needed a nap,' he said. 'Now, decision time. Do you have to go back to the nurses' home straight away? Would you like to stay for a little? We could have an easy night. Have something to eat, watch TV or listen to some music, just take it easy in general.'

'Sounds good to me,' she said.

So they just sat there, clicking through TV channels and not watching anything for very long. After a while he fetched them a sandwich each, and even a little pot of leftover jelly. After their snack she kicked off her shoes and lay across his lap.

'I like being here with you,' she said. 'I don't feel I have to talk to you all the time. Though I like talking. But I feel at home just being with you. I'm comfortable with you.'

'I'm comfortable with you, too,' he said, and stretched his arm round her waist.

For both of them it was a calm evening. Later on he said he wanted to try his present, and fetched two glasses.

'It's not very much for two people,' she said. 'Perhaps I should have bought a bigger bottle. But I wanted it to be just for you.'

'And I want to share,' he said. 'Please drink it.'

So she sipped the smoky liquid and she liked it. 'I seldom drink spirits,' she said, 'just the occasional gin with lots of tonic. But this is nice.'

'We'll open a bottle of wine later,' he said.

Gently, the evening ebbed away. She was happy just lying there—but she was aware that soon it would be bedtime, time for another, much greater decision. And it was he who brought the subject up.

'Do you have to go?' he asked.

To Jane's surprise the answer came out without her thinking about it. 'Not if I'm asked to stay.'

'You know how much I want you to stay.' His voice was low.

Yes, she knew. And she knew that her mind was made up. But... 'Remember we talked not so long ago,' she said, 'and we said that...that when we made love it was largely physical? Something that just overwhelmed us?'

'*You* said that it was just physical. I didn't.'

'Well, I needed to say that. To think that. But this is the second time. I've got time to think and consider. It'll be...' She couldn't think of or say the words.

'It'll be some kind of commitment,' he said.

'I suppose so. But I'm scared, Chris.'

'I'm scared myself. Let's go to bed and be scared together.'

'I want to go to bed with you.' She had said it.

He kissed her, gently at first, and then traced his finger down the side of her face, over her chin and into the opening of her shirt. He smiled. 'I suspect that down here there's more than a bit of jelly. That Polly child managed to spread it everywhere. Would you like a bath?'

'I think it might be a good idea. But I've no nightie and no toothbrush.'

'I'll lend you a toothbrush. And who needs a nightie? Now, just wait here a minute.'

He left, she heard him walking upstairs. She felt surprisingly calm. She had made up her mind, there was no going back now. How things would work out she just didn't know. But for the moment…things felt right.

He came down in a dark silk dressing-gown. He took both her hands, raised her from the couch and kissed her on the lips. 'Last time was wonderful but perhaps we were in too much of a hurry,' he said softly. 'Trying to grab what we could, afraid that the chance might disappear. Now I want to take all the time we have. I want to enjoy you.'

'We're going to enjoy each other,' she said.

He took her to his bedroom and, as she stood facing him, undid the buttons of her shirt and carefully slipped it off. He undid her bra—a lacy one this time. Then he bent his head to kiss her breasts and when his lips touched her hardened nipples she sobbed with excitement.

'Lovely,' he said. 'Like I said, that jelly gets everywhere. Tangerine flavour, my favourite.'

She sighed, sadly. 'I've always wanted a great romantic as a lover.'

Her shoes were already kicked off. With precision, and very slowly, he undid the belt of her trousers, eased them down to her ankles. She stepped out of them. Then she gasped as his fingers slowly inserted themselves inside her skimpy briefs. She flinched with excitement at his touch as he slid them downwards. Now she was naked. And she loved it.

'You're wearing too many clothes,' she told him. 'I want you to be like me.' With fumbling fingers she pushed aside his dressing-gown, dropped it to the floor. Now he too was naked, and she gloried in his maleness. She leaned towards him, and the first intimate touch of skin on skin was magic.

'Not yet,' he murmured, 'not for a while yet. Come with me, I've got you a small surprise.'

He led her by the hand to the bathroom—she blinked. Six candles round the room flickered and were reflected by what seemed to be a multitude of mirrors. The bath was full, steaming, with some kind of sweet-smelling foam on top. He took her hand, helped her to step in. 'Just the right temperature,' she said.

He grinned. 'I can bathe babies. I tested the temperature with my elbow.'

It was fun for a while just to lie there, with him kneeling by the side of the bath, squeezing water over her shoulders from a dinosaur-shaped sponge. She felt her previous weariness drain away. And with the weariness went the slight apprehension. Now she knew she would be able to give herself fully to him.

He covered the sponge with some kind of soft liquid soap, and with his hand on her back washed her.

Having her breasts washed by him was more than sexual—it brought a pleasure that reminded her of her childhood. Then he washed the rest of her body. She lay there like an Eastern potentate, languorously extending him an arm or a leg for him to wash and rinse. She loved it.

Finally, she was ready to get out. He helped her to stand, then showered away all the foam that clung to her body. As she stepped from the bath there was a giant blue towel for her to wrap herself in.

'We're not wasting all that foam,' she said. 'Now it's your turn to get in. And I'll wash you.' So he climbed into the bath, and in her turn she washed him.

'Now to the bedroom,' he said.

They sat in bed and drank a glass of chilled champagne each. He poured some onto her breast, she shivered with the cold. Then he leaned over to lick the stickiness away, and she shivered for a totally different reason.

Time passed and they were in no hurry. But each understood that there was something to come, but that all would be well.

Finally it was she who pulled him on top of her, urging his body towards hers, opening herself to receive him. Their love-making was prolonged, sweet. Perhaps it lacked the fire and desperation of the first time, but in its languor it was…not better but different.

It was wonderful to discover his body, to find out what he liked, the things she could do that would make him moan with desperation and passion. And he made the same discoveries about her. There were so many places to kiss, so much to stroke and caress. So much pleasure to be taken and given. And finally, when they reached that joint sobbing climax, the long wait had been worthwhile. Now they would sleep together.

'One thing,' she murmured. 'I still must be gone before James wakes. We don't want him knowing about us.'

He didn't answer at once, she could tell he was thinking about it. 'Perhaps so,' he said. 'But I want to tell him soon. Very soon.' Then they both slept.

It was very early Sunday morning but Jane had things to do. Sunday was usually washing day, so Jane collected her basket of clothes and went down to the communal laundry room in the basement. Because she was early, there was no one else there. So she filled the machine, selected the programme and then sat to watch frilly little pink and white things revolving.

She heard footsteps coming towards her and to her surprise Erica walked in with an equally large basket of washing. 'I couldn't sleep,' she said, 'so I decided to get up and do some work.' She smiled at Jane weakly. 'I take it that you have just got in?'

'My guilty secret,' Jane said with a little grin. 'Though this is a hospital and I don't think it will be a secret for long.'

'Not long,' Erica agreed. 'I hope things are going well for you.' Suddenly she grabbed for her pocket, took out a handkerchief and held it to her eyes. 'Better than they're going for me.'

Jane strode over to her friend, put her arms round her shoulders. 'You're in trouble again,' she said. 'Come on, tell me all. Things are better when you've talked about them.'

Erica sniffed, wiped her eyes. Then she shook herself and said in a stronger voice, 'It's just that I'm a fool. And now I know it. Martin phoned and nearly tricked me yesterday and I should have known better.'

'What happened?'

'He phoned me yesterday morning, and he was all right. He said he was phoning to apologise, that he realised that his behaviour had been unforgivable but he at least wanted to say he was sorry. Then he said he'd had the offer of a new job, had decided to give up drinking and already his life looked better. He missed me so much but I must get on with my own life.'

'Did you believe him?' Jane asked.

'Well, I did a bit. And I said I'd have a think and that he could call me later.'

'Were you thinking of going back to him?' Jane asked neutrally. She knew that the last thing she should do was offer advice, people had to make up their own minds. But sometimes it was hard not to.

'No, I wasn't thinking of going back to him. He phoned at seven. Told me to ring for a taxi and come and join him down at the Fisherman's Rest. His voice was both slurred and cocky, he'd obviously been drinking. He said I was to pack a bag with a few clothes, I wouldn't be going back to the nurses' home that night. A friend had lent him a flat, we could be alone together. I said I didn't think so. Then he started shouting, said we'd sorted all this out this morning, what was wrong with me? So I rang off. He rang right back, told me what would happen to me if I didn't listen to him. We were meant to be together, I knew that and he was going to prove it.'

Now the tears were running down Erica's face. 'Jane, how could I have been so wrong?'

Jane tried to comfort her friend, wrapping her arms round her. 'There's nothing much I can say,' she said. 'Well, just one thing. Problems do pass. You can be happy again in time.'

Erica made another valiant attempt to control herself. 'I know that really. Compared with you, I've had an easy time. I shouldn't feel so sorry for myself.'

'You're entitled to feel sorry,' said Jane. 'Now, if you carry on crying you'll look terrible. Why don't you go and have a long bath? It always helps me. I'll see to all your washing and bring it up when it's done.'

'You will? But—'

'Just go,' said Jane, flapping her hands at her friend. 'We'll have a mid-morning coffee together when it's done.'

Erica did go, and Jane busied herself sorting the washing into piles. She felt so sorry for Erica. But then she wondered about what her friend had said. Only three months before she had been happy, contented with her partner, expecting to spend the rest of her life with him. And now this. Her partner, her home, most of her savings, all gone. And she was being stalked at the same time.

Jane thought of herself, only a few short weeks before, resolute in her determination never to look at another man. And now she was thinking of... Perhaps she was in too much of a hurry. There was so much about Chris she didn't know. She might be rushing into even more heartache.

This morning she had woken so cheerful, now she was nearly depressed. Only one thing to do.

Chris had told her that this morning he was taking James to see some old family friends. Jane rang him on his mobile and caught him just before they left. 'Jane! It's good to hear from you.'

The moment she heard his voice she felt better. It was warm, friendly. It was loving. 'I've got a problem,' she said. 'I know all I want is reassurance, but it's still a problem. I've just been talking to Erica and...' She told him the full story. Then she added, 'And so I'm wondering if I might change the way I feel about you. Or you might change the way I feel about me.'

He listened to her without interruption and he didn't take her worries lightly. 'There's always a chance that relationships might go wrong,' he said. 'Don't I know it. And at the moment I'm trying not to push you—or me—into anything that we might regret. We'll take things easy. But I want you to know something. I think you are the biggest chance of happiness I will ever get. And I hope you feel the same about me.'

'I do.'

'Good. Now, shall we have a small celebration ourselves? Dinner at the Escott next Wednesday?'

'That'll be lovely. Something to look forward to.' She felt better.

There was one small extra pleasure for Jane on Wednesday. Matt had been working in one of the other rooms with Erica. Jane had always got on well with Matt, all the nurses liked him. But there was now something new between him and Erica.

Nothing too obvious. He talked to her rather longer than was necessary. They laughed gently together.

When they bent to look at something, their shoulders touched.

And there was a great change in Erica, something in her body language. Her shoulders no longer stooped, her eyes sparkled, she didn't look defeated any more. Jane thought that Erica was feeling like a whole woman again.

Jane walked back to the nurses' home with Erica later. 'You've looked a happy bunny today,' she teased her friend, 'I don't think I've seen you smile so much since I met you.'

Erica turned rather pink. 'We're just friends,' she said. 'Well, we've been sort of friends for ages and…well, I don't know. But I do like him.'

'How come he's not been snapped up by some smart-moving nurse before? He's good-looking, ever so kind.' Jane frowned as something struck her. 'He hasn't got a nasty history behind him, has he? Some woman he now hates or who hates him?'

'No, nothing like that.' Erica shook her head vigorously. 'He's been living with his father, looking after him, in fact. He was the centre of Matt's life. But a couple of weeks ago the old man died—and Matt's now finding himself with a new life to lead.'

'Was he very upset when his father died?'

'In a way,' Erica said. 'But it was expected and in many ways it was a release.'

'I see,' said Jane. 'And so now…'

'Just a minute,' Erica said. 'I'm not the only one round here who looks as if she's just had a double birthday. You've got starlight in your eyes, Jane. It can't be the job, that's still a pain. Either it's the local food or the sea air or something else entirely, but you

look worlds different from when you first came up
here. You look happy. You know you used to have
lines on your face where you frowned? Well, they've
gone.'

'I'm eating too well,' Jane said, and giggled.

CHAPTER SEVEN

IT WAS an hour before Chris was due to call for her and although she was ravenous she fought the temptation to have something to eat. The food at the Escott was wonderful—she was determined to do it justice.

So she showered, noticed that her blonde hair was now growing out even more. Soon she would have to decide on a new style. When she'd been eleven she'd had long blonde plaits swinging down her back. No, perhaps not this time.

She put on lacy white underwear, a pretty blue dress. Decided it was too warm to wear tights but that her legs were now tanned enough. She took extra care with her make-up, she was going to look good. Then she heard a ring at the door downstairs. None of the other girls was expecting anyone so it must be Chris, a bit earlier than he had said. She ran down to let him in.

The evening sun was shining through the marbled glass door and all she could see was the vague silhouette of a male form. She bent to undo the lock and threw open the door. She was glad he was early, they could sit in her room a while and... It wasn't Chris. It was Martin Berry—Erica's ex-partner.

Jane looked at him in horror. 'You can't come in,' she said. 'Just go away or I'll call Security and...' She tried to close the door in his face.

He was too quick for her. He stepped forward,

pushed her to one side. 'Who says I can't come in?' he snarled. 'Who's going to stop me? I'm seeing Erica and you can get out of my way.' He slammed the door shut behind him.

Jane felt the first touch of fear. The man stank of drink, he looked wild, as if he didn't know what he was doing. But she didn't like being pushed and she had dealt with awkward men before when she'd worked in A and E.

'You mind who you're pushing,' she snapped. 'I told you you weren't coming in. If you want to talk to Erica you can—'

The man started yelling. 'Erica! Erica! It's no good trying to hide from me, I won't have it. I know you're up there and I'm coming to see you. We're going to talk whether you like it or not. No one treats me this way, you're going to find that out.'

From his pocket he took a bottle and drank from it, and the smell of cheap spirits filled the air.

Another voice came down the stairwell. It was Erica, and Jane could tell that she was terrified. 'Jane…Martin…what is it? What are you doing here?'

Martin's voice was now a screech, and Jane realised with horror that he was far more than drunk. He was demented, screaming like a banshee.

'I've come for you, you're going with me right now. I don't care what you want and if you really want trouble then it's coming to you.'

Jane knew she couldn't let him get to Erica in this state. As he seized the banister and prepared to climb the stairs, she managed to get in front of him and said, 'I told you, you can't—'

Perhaps she should have expected it but she didn't.

He hit her. A great round-arm sweep that caught her on the side of the face, knocked her over so that she fell on her side on a step.

She felt a crack, then a pain that engulfed her, became the centre of her life, there was nothing for her but pain. All she could do was lie there, perfectly still, holding herself. Perhaps soon the pain would go away. It pulsed through her body in great sickening waves.

But slowly other things seemed to intrude. There were screams from above her. He had caught Erica, what was he doing to her? And there was another noise, a hammering, a banging. In front of her there was another figure outlined against the glass of the door, hitting it with his fist and shouting. Martin had shut the door. It must be Chris outside, trying to get in. But he couldn't. He could hear the screams, the shouting, perhaps see her vague outline on the stairs. But he couldn't get in.

She would have to unlock the door.

It was the hardest thing she had ever done. It was no good just lying here. Somehow she would have to get to the door, open it so Chris could get in. But she didn't want to move. She knew if she moved that it would hurt, and she didn't want to hurt more. But she had to.

She rolled over and, just as she had expected, the pain lanced through her. Probably a rib broken. She hoped it wouldn't pierce something vital. She had to move! No way could she stand up. So she crawled. How far to the door? Only a few feet, but it seemed to take her an age, and the pain was growing, growing... But she got there. One last effort to reach up to unlock the door. And then it clicked open and she rolled back, sobbing. She had done what she could.

Chris dragged open the door, stepped inside. She caught a quick glimpse of his appalled face. Then he knelt by her side, reached for her head. She had to get her message across.

'Please,' she managed to croak, 'I'm all right. Leave me for now. Go and see to Erica, he might kill her.'

She could see the indecision in his face. 'What has he done to you? I—'

He bent further over her. She managed to shout, even louder. 'Are you listening to me? I said I was all right now go and look after Erica!' Then, mysteriously, in the middle of her agony she managed to say, 'I'm not going anywhere.'

She saw the indecision disappear. Swiftly, he bent his head, kissed her tear-stained cheek, then he was gone.

There were mists swirling through her brain now. Jane decided she'd done all she could fairly be asked to do. Now she could feel sorry for herself. In fact, she could faint. She was entitled to. So she fainted.

She had worked in the A and E department of a hospital. She knew that after an accident or some sudden trauma people could apparently be awake but dazed, fearful, knowing what was happening but incapable of dealing with it. Now she knew what it really felt like.

All she could do was lie there. Upstairs there was screaming, shouting, the crashing of furniture. It wasn't her concern. She was out of it now. She would just lie here and deal with the pain.

Then, from somewhere, Chris was with her again,

kneeling by her side. Her vision was blurred but she managed to force open her eyes, stare at him. He was so close. She could read his expression, there was horror and an overwhelming concern. And love?

But then his face changed and she saw that by a terrific effort of will he was turning himself from a lover into a doctor. 'You're going to be all right,' he said. 'I've phoned A and E, they're sending a trolley over, it's not far. Now, don't try to move your head, don't move, don't try to talk for a minute.'

His fingers were on her head, testing her jaw, feeling her skull, her upper spine, trying to determine if there were any fractures. A finger caressed her cheek, she knew she was going to get a tremendous bruise there.

'Now, where's it hurt most?'

'My head hurts a lot but mostly it's my side. I think I've broken a rib.' There was something she had to know. 'How's Erica?'

'She's fine. Shaken a bit, but you're hurt a lot worse.' Professionally he unbuttoned the front of her dress then eased his hand down her side. Suddenly the pain returned, as strong as before. 'Ow,' she said.

Then she realised there was something else she had to know, and fear clouded her eyes. She couldn't say Martin's name. ' Him,' she said. 'He came for Erica. What happened to him?' She knew her voice was trembling, but she desperately needed to know.

'He'll be no trouble,' Chris said dismissively. 'I've dealt with him.'

She was glad about that. So Erica was all right and Chris was here and the pain was still there but she didn't need to worry any more. Perhaps it was time to shut her eyes again. 'My side still hurts,' she said.

She knew that Chris was holding her hand. But after a while he took it away and there were other voices, a set of tender hands holding her, taking her, lifting her onto something. Then a couple of bumps and she was outside! She could feel the coolness of a breeze on her cheeks, the glare of the sun on her closed eyelids.

She was in A and E. She passed straight through Triage into a cubicle. Nurses, some of whom she vaguely recognised, were undressing her. She heard one tell Chris to wait outside. Her pretty blue dress was torn and dirty. Pity, that.

She knew what was happening, was content to just lie there and have things done to her. Her head and neck were X-rayed, no cause for concern. Her back was X-rayed, yes, a broken rib and considerable bruising. Then she was given painkillers, her face was gently washed, her rib strapped up and she was allowed to rest. What a good idea! She could sleep. But as she dozed she felt someone sit beside her, take her hand in his.

When she woke Chris was sent out and a ludicrously young doctor and an older nurse came in to look at her. 'How d'you feel?' asked the doctor, as he took her pulse.

She thought. 'Hungry,' she said. 'I haven't had anything to eat since breakfast.'

The doctor and nurse exchanged glances. 'It'll be hard, eating with a bruised mouth,' said the nurse, 'but I could fetch you a warm drink with something in it.'

'I'd like that. And there's another thing. I'm not taking up a bed here all night. I want to go back to my own room.'

The doctor looked doubtful. 'You're not too badly injured,' he said, 'but you've had a nasty shock and I think we'd like to keep an eye on you overnight.'

'Perhaps we could think about it when you've had your drink,' said the nurse. 'You might have got more of your strength back then. And you've got a visitor outside.'

That's a good nurse, Jane thought.

Sitting up was hard and painful, but the nurse and doctor helped her, packed pillows behind her back. Then they left and Chris came in. He sat by her bed, took her hand in his. 'I was terrified,' he said. 'I saw you there on the floor and I was terrified.'

She said, 'If I turn my head you can kiss my other cheek. The non-damaged one.'

'I'd like that.' So he kissed her. Then he sat there, holding her hand.

'I'm feeling better,' she said. 'I need to know what happened. How's Erica?'

'Not too bad. Not hurt as badly as you. But she's very upset so they've brought her in here and given her a sedative and they're going to keep her overnight. Tomorrow she'll be fine. And that's largely because of you.'

She knew her voice would tremble but she had to ask. 'And…and that man? What happened to him? Has he got away?'

'No.'

Just one syllable. Jane looked at him and thought he was looking decidedly shifty. 'Come on,' she said. 'You're keeping something from me. I told you, I need to know.'

'He's here in A and E, too. There's a policeman

sitting outside his door and when he's discharged the police will arrest him for assault. Apparently he's got up to quite a bit in the past few weeks.'

'Why is he in A and E?'

Chris looked more embarrassed than ever. 'He's got a broken jaw. I hit him a bit too hard.'

She had to giggle. 'Mr Fielding! Violence towards a disturbed man.'

'I'll give him disturbed. Besides, he was trying to hit me with a bottle. I could have been killed.' He bent over, kissed her gently on the lips. 'And to hell with being a doctor. When I see what he's done to you I'd like to hit him again.'

'Do I look a mess?'

'No. You look like a woman who's just fought for her friend.'

This was all very nice, but there were things she had to say. 'Chris, you know I'm not that badly hurt. I want to go back to my room. I'm a fraud, staying here.'

'You're not a fraud. But I'll have a word with that young doctor and see what he thinks. We'll negotiate.'

'I've seen you negotiating,' she said. 'Be gentle with him. Oh, and there's one more thing.'

'Anything.'

'Phone Matt and tell him what's happened and that Erica's in A and E.'

'Tell Matt? Why should he…? Oh, Erica?' He grinned. 'Oh, I see. All right, then, I will.'

He left, and shortly afterwards the young doctor appeared. 'I want one last look at you,' he said, 'and then I've been persuaded to release you into Mr Fielding's care. Just one thing, and it's very important.

You've had quite a knock so take it easy for at least three days. And you have a week off work. OK?'

'OK,' said Jane. Another one who is young but good, she thought.

There was a wheelchair to take her to the entrance—she hated it but she knew they were right to insist. Chris was waiting for her there with his car. Gently she was eased into it and they made the short run to the nurses' home. He supported her as they went to the lift, up to her floor and along to her room. Then he helped her lie on her bed, and there, for the first time, she cried. She didn't know why.

He held her gently, tenderly, and said nothing. And when she'd finished he fetched her a damp flannel, and the coolness on her face made her feel much better.

'There's not enough room in this bed for two,' he said, 'especially if one has a broken rib or two. But I want to stay with you. Is that all right?'

'Yes, but where will you—?'

'I'll sleep on the floor. I've done it plenty of times before. I just want to be with you, be where I can hold your hand.'

'That's lovely.' She knew she would sleep soon, she felt safe, comforted, and the powerful painkillers she had been given were making her drowsy. Then her eyes jerked open. Just one more thing to ask. 'Erica? Did you phone Matt?'

'I did. And for the first time ever he asked me to do him a favour. Could I arrange for him to be off call for tonight and all of tomorrow? I arranged it. I don't think he plans on moving far from Erica's bedside.'

'That's nice,' she said. 'I think I'm going to sleep now. Just one more thing?'

'Yes?'

'You owe me a meal at the Escott Arms.'

Waking up next morning was strange. Jane's body didn't want to wake, knew it was better off asleep. But slowly she came to consciousness and lay there without moving, eyes closed, taking an inventory of her aches and pains. She was stiff, she was sore, she was surprisingly tired. But she was alive.

After a while she opened her eyes and slowly turned her head. There was Chris, asleep on her floor. He was lying on the cushions from her easy chair, had made a pillow from his clothes and was lying under her thick dressing-gown. One muscular arm reached limply out to where he had been holding her hand, the other was behind his head.

She had never looked at him closely while he was asleep. He looked unusually relaxed—younger, sweeter almost. The harsh lines that sometime spoilt his face were gone. He looked happier.

He must have felt her gaze. His eyes flicked open and he was instantly alert. 'Good morning, sweetheart. How do you feel?'

He'd never called her sweetheart before. She rather liked it. But the question he had put to her had been that of a doctor. 'I feel stiff, sore and sleepy,' she told him, 'but I did sleep well.'

Apparently this wasn't too bad an answer. 'Mother Nature taking her course,' he said. 'You'll get better quicker if you sleep a lot. How about if I help you to your bathroom, make you breakfast and then you rest and I go to work?'

Something suddenly struck her, something she

hadn't thought of before. 'Chris! What about James? You've been with me all night and he—'

'No need to worry. I phoned Mrs Mansell last night and she was only too pleased to stay the night and send him off to playschool this morning. I'll call in to see him later. Now, you're to get up, but very slowly.'

He helped her to the bathroom and she nearly wept when she saw her face in the bathroom mirror. A great bruise covered her cheek and puffed up her left eye. She looked a mess! But the nurse in her recognised that the damage was only superficial and would pass very quickly. There would be no long-term damage.

'You can go now,' she told him. 'I'm all right but I want to be alone. If you want to make some breakfast then the key to my locker in the kitchen is on the table.'

He was still a doctor. He looked at her assessingly for a moment, then obviously decided she was fit to be left. 'I'll be back in exactly fifteen minutes,' he said.

When he had gone she managed to wriggle out of her nightie, sponge herself down and clean her teeth. It was all right so long as she didn't make any sudden movements or try to bend awkwardly. Then she found herself another nightie and was sitting propped up in bed when he returned.

He placed a tray in front of her. 'I've been overwhelmed with enquiries,' he said. 'Assorted nurses, all in different states of undress. No one seemed to be upset at seeing me there. There's a lot of goodwill towards you, everyone wants to help, but I told them that the best thing to do was to leave you alone to sleep all morning. A couple down the corridor say they're off today and if you want anything you're just to shout. Now, breakfast.'

He'd cooked her porridge, which she liked and which was quite easy to eat with her bruised mouth. Then she had tea and felt considerably better—but also sleepy. 'You can go now,' she said. 'I'm going to be all right.'

'I think you are. But first I'm going to pretend I'm a doctor and give you a quick examination.'

As he'd said, it was just a quick examination but it proved that she was more or less all right. And surely most examinations didn't end with the doctor kissing the patient? Still...

'I think you're OK,' he said. 'I gather a nurse will call later to look at the strapping on your ribs, but all you really need now is rest. I'll be back. But it might not be until this evening.'

'I'll be fine,' she said, 'but you're confusing me.'

He looked upset. 'Confusing you? How?'

'You keep on swapping jobs. I don't know whether you're my doctor or my lover.'

He frowned and gave it some thought. 'Being your doctor means that I can pretend that I'm at a distance from you. If I'd only been your lover then I don't know how I would have coped with seeing you like this.'

She had only meant her comment as a little joke but it struck her then that, yes, he had suffered. In his way possibly as much as she had. 'I think you're lovely,' she said. 'Now go away and let me sleep.'

She dozed again. At lunchtime a nurse called and checked her strapping and general health. A girl down the corridor asked if she should bring some lunch in and Jane had more tea and a bowl of soup. Then, surprisingly, she cried because everyone was so good to her. And afterwards she realised that she was still upset, so she slept some more.

When she awoke at teatime she felt considerably better. There was a text message on her mobile phone by her bed. It was from Chris. 'Don't eat, I'll bring a picnic meal later. I'll get someone else to let me in.'

A picnic meal? Great. It struck her she was really hungry. Which was odd since all she'd done all day had been to sleep and eat a little. Then, painfully, she eased herself out of bed and put on yet another nightie—not a high-necked, comfortable nightie like the one she was taking off, but a pretty, lacy one that showed rather a lot of cleavage. Well, why not?

She fetched her make-up bag and brushed her hair. There wasn't a lot she could do about her face—if anything, the bruising looked even worse— but she put on a touch of make-up and felt better for it. Then she waited for Chris. She had things to say.

He came after he'd been home. Even though Mrs Mansell was staying another night, he'd wanted to see James. Jane heard the bustle in the hall outside, guessed that he had been let in. And then he was in her room, carrying parcels and an insulated box that gave off a remarkably savoury smell.

He kissed her. She held up a finger and said, 'Before we go any further, let's get one thing straight. I know I'm fine and I'm going to get better. The nurse has been, she says I'm fine. So tonight you're not in any way my doctor. OK?'

'What is there left for me to be? Just your lover?' He smiled.

'There's no ''just'' in being a lover. Now, I'm ravenous but before we start, how's Erica? I thought she might have come in to see me. She hasn't had any kind of relapse?'

He grinned. 'Not at all. Whatever the opposite of relapse is—upsurge or advancement or something— Erica has had one. And all because of you. When it comes to plotting you're cunning and devious. I hadn't realised that, Sister Wilson.'

'Come on, what's happened?'

'I told you I phoned Matt and he asked for the day off. It now turns out that he has moved Erica into his house. In case she was worried about coming back here.'

'Of course,' said Jane.

'All quite proper. Matt has several spare bedrooms. I'm sure nothing…improper will happen. And I don't think she'll be in a hurry to move back here.'

'You know,' said Jane, 'quite a lot of good has come out of that lunatic's actions.' Then she shivered, thinking of how her side had hurt. 'What's happening to him, by the way?'

'He's been taken away by the police, kept in custody. I've made a statement and I told them that you were too ill to be interviewed. With any luck you won't have to say anything. There's a suggestion that he might need psychiatric attention, not a trial and then a prison sentence.'

'Just so long as he keeps away from Erica.'

'Just so long as he keeps away from you,' Chris said softly. 'Anyway, it's out of our hands now.'

He was pulling plates and packages out of his carrier bags, arranging them on her table. It looked rather a lot for a picnic—but she did feel hungry. He fetched plates from her locker then opened the insulated box.

'Mrs Mansell was very upset to hear you had been hurt,' he said. 'She believes that good food is better than medicine for getting people better so she's sent you her speciality. Chicken, bean and new potato stew.' He spooned it onto two plates, then handed her one.

'Oh, wow!' said Jane.

It was a great picnic. And to finish he popped open a bottle of champagne. She loved champagne!

'That meal was fantastic,' she said. 'Chris, everyone's been so good to me, and now I feel so much better. I've slept all day but now I'm getting a bit fed up with it so I'll get up and—'

He pressed her back onto her pillows. 'No question,' he said. 'I'll clear up. Then we'll just sit here and have a peaceful evening.'

'Perhaps not too peaceful,' she said. 'I've got things to say.'

He looked at her, rather cautiously, she thought. 'Just a doctor idea,' he said. 'You might be still a little upset by what has happened. Is this a good time to make decisions?'

'It's the best time. Getting knocked down by that lout has made me see things a bit differently.'

'Well, if you're sure. But I'll certainly clear up first.'

While he was out of the room she slipped into her bathroom, cleaned her teeth, tidied herself a little more. Then she climbed back into bed, tried to compose herself. What she had to say was important and she felt a little afraid. But she was going to say it.

He came back, sat in the chair by her bed, looked at her carefully again. She picked up her half-empty champagne flute, held it towards him. 'May I have a refill, please?' she asked.

He poured more sparkling wine into her glass and his. Then she leaned forward, clinked their glasses together. 'I don't often do this,' she said, 'but today might be special, so here's a toast. To a happy future.'

'To a happy future,' he echoed, and drank. But she could tell he was still wary.

'I haven't slept all today,' she told him. 'I've had times when I've just lain here and thought. About me and about you and about the future.'

He looked more worried than ever. 'Are you sure this is a good time for this kind of talk? You know you could be still a little disturbed.'

'It's because I've been disturbed that I want to say this.' She swallowed, discovered to her surprise that she was near tears. 'That fight yesterday. He just pushed me. But you told me that he tried to hit you with a bottle. You could have been killed. I've seen people bleeding to death in A and E after being hit by bottles.'

'But I wasn't killed! He didn't hit me and—'

'That's not the point! The point is you could have been killed. Perhaps you were just lucky.'

'Jane, it's finished, there's no need to go over it again. Don't dwell on it.'

'I have to. Because I think it's taught me something.' She took a breath. This was important, she had to get it just right. 'My husband died and I decided never again to risk any emotional entanglements. The chances of getting hurt were just too great. Then I met you and…I quite liked you. But I was afraid of getting too close, getting hurt again. Then that night… I didn't expect it but something…my body perhaps…betrayed me.' She smiled. 'Though it was a lovely betrayal.'

'It was lovely indeed,' he said.

'Well, now I'm changing my ideas. Whatever life has to offer, I'm going to grab. You never can know what might happen, so why not just hope? There's a Latin phrase we learned at school—*Carpe diem*. Seize the day. So that's what I'm going to do from now on.'

'And am I part of this plan?' he asked quietly.

'I hope so. If you want to be. But I suspect you're as nervous as I am. Frightened of commitment.'

He stood and walked over to the window, stared out at the parkland below. 'I've been just like you,' he said. 'Perhaps in a way that's what brought us together. After my wife left I thought of nothing but James and my work. Women just weren't worth the effort or the risk. Now it's time for me to change, just like you are doing. I'm willing to risk being hurt again. That way I'm likely to be happy.'

'Both of us,' said Jane. 'From now on we're going to live—not just exist.'

CHAPTER EIGHT

AFTER three days in her room Jane thought she'd go mad. She'd read all the magazines people had brought her, listened to the radio, watched afternoon television and tried to draw up a plan for the future of the ward. Evenings were all right—no, evenings were wonderful as Chris called. But she insisted that he go back home to look after James.

It was no good. She had to be active. On the morning of the fourth day she phoned her doctor. 'I've just got to go back to the ward,' she said. 'Doing nothing is driving me mad.'

'I'll come round and have a quick look at you.'

He examined her, checked her notes. Then he said, 'You're pushing me and I'm not sure this is right. You've had a big shock to the system, you should rest more. But doing what you want is probably just better than getting restless at home. Go into the ward if you like. But no lifting. No bending. In fact, no nursing, you're fit for light clerical work only. Is that a bargain?'

'I'll do as you say,' Jane said. She went back that afternoon.

It was good to be back in harness. The attitude of the other nurses interested her. Everyone knew about what had happened, of course. She was treated with more respect, more affection even, than before. And everyone was running round, trying to do her jobs.

'Look,' she said, as she accepted yet another coffee in the nurses' room, 'I've got a bruised face and a broken rib. I am not an invalid, I can still work.'

'You do more than most ward managers,' a nurse said. 'Just take it easy for a week or so and just do what's considered enough by other people.'

It was part of her job but it was surprisingly hard. She had to teach the younger nurses. And when she supervised one, slowly doing something that she could have done in a quarter of the time herself, it was hard not just to take over. But young nurses had to learn.

Now Sue was helping Matt introduce an umbilical catheter. She was slow, but careful and methodical. And Matt was happy for her to take her time. Eventually it was done. Sue stared at the fine plastic tube. 'I suppose it's the obvious way to feed a baby,' she said. 'He's been getting nourishment that way for months. But it still looks odd.'

'It's often a lifesaver,' Matt said. 'You did a good job.'

'You can go for a break,' Jane added. 'you're looking a bit shaken.'

'I am,' said Sue.

'Well, that was fun while it lasted,' Jane said to Matt when they shared a coffee afterwards. 'Now, tell me how Erica's getting on.'

The SHO blushed. 'Chris says I'm to thank you for letting me know she'd been hurt,' he said. 'How did you know that I…that we…?'

'Like a good doctor, a good nurse is observant,'

Jane said drily. 'I can tell when people are attracted to each other.'

Matt grinned. 'I'll bet you know all about what it feels like to be attracted, and when you can't do much about it,' he said, and then it was her turn to blush.

'So how is she?'

'Erica is improving. You know she's taken a few days' holiday. She's not physically hurt so much but she's quite shaken up still. Her doctor has prescribed tranquillisers for a week because she's not sleeping very well. Would you like to come over tonight for supper to say hello? I know she'd love to see you.'

'And I'd love to see her. What time shall I arrive?'

'About nine? I'll pick you up and bring you back. In fact, you can help me a little. Erica wants some things from her room.'

'I'm glad she's planning a long stay with you,' Jane said cheerfully.

She explained to Chris what she was doing, then told him that he was not to come to see her that night. He was to spend the evening with James. He thought it a good idea. 'But I'll be back tomorrow night,' he said.

Matt called just before nine, with the key to Erica's room and a list of things to bring. Jane helped him select and pack, was rather surprised at the amount Erica had asked for. She wondered if her friend planned on staying away from the nurses' home for good. 'When might Erica be coming back?' she asked Matt casually.

'Never, if I have anything to do with it. She can stay with me as long as she wants. I really like having her around, she makes the house seem alive. And it's not been that for ages.'

'Erica is terrific,' said Jane. She decided not to say any more.

Erica was horrified when she saw the bruise on Jane's cheek, even though it was now much better than it had been. And Jane was a little shaken by Erica. Her friend had obviously been shocked by what had happened. There were dark shadows under her eyes and apprehension in the way she looked round at any unexpected noise. But Jane noticed that when she looked at Matt there was love and happiness in her gaze. And Matt was clearly devoted. Whenever he could he touched her hand, her shoulder, her arms. And the two smiled at each other in that self-contained way that Jane loved.

Matt went to prepare their supper. Erica went to a side table, took up a set of paint samples and swatches of material. 'You can help me,' she said. 'I'm helping Matt decide how to decorate this place. It's not been done for ages, you can see how it needs brightening up.'

'True,' said Jane, who had been thinking just that.

'I thought,' said Erica, going slightly red, 'that I'd start with the main bedroom. What about this for curtains—and this for the walls? There's quite a nice red carpet down already.'

'Looks lovely,' said Jane. 'Erica, are you planning on staying here?'

'I haven't been asked. But if I am asked, and I think it's likely, I'll say yes.'

'You don't feel scared? After what happened with Martin?'

'Matt isn't Martin. And in this life you've got to take chances.'

Just what I was saying yesterday, Jane thought. Interesting that the same accident caused us both to think the same way.

'Anyway,' Erica went on with a twinkle in her eye, 'what's this about you having a man stay the night in your room? Do I gather that you're going to have a happy ending, too?'

'Possibly,' said Jane, 'just possibly.'

Recently Fiona had been keeping a very low profile so Jane was surprised when next day she asked if she could see her for a few minutes.

'I've been thinking about what you said about us all furthering our careers,' she said. 'And I want to do something myself.'

She pushed some printed sheets across to Jane. 'There's this six-month course in London that would give me a diploma in the use of the latest paediatric techniques. It would make me a better qualified, more proficient children's nurse. I'd like to go on it.'

Jane scanned the sheets. It was a good course at a reputable university hospital. 'I'd like you to go on it,' she said, 'but I don't think there's any way we can pay your salary while you do it.'

'I know that and I've got some money saved. I've asked Human Resources here, they say that they'll give me leave of absence for six months and keep my job open. They will pay my fees if I sign to say that I'll come back here for at least three years.'

'Well, that's great. I'll be pleased to write you any reference you might need.'

'Actually, there's another thing,' Fiona said, looking uneasy. 'It's hard to get on this course but someone has dropped out. I can have a place—but it starts in a week.'

'A week! How can I replace you in a week? Couldn't you have let me know before?'

'I've only just found out about the extra place,' said Fiona.

Jane sighed. 'Come back and see me in an hour,' she said. 'I'll phone Human Resources.'

Human Resources said that they could arrange for Fiona to go on the course, but the ultimate decision was Jane's. She would be fully within her rights to tell Fiona it just wasn't possible to release her. On the other hand, when Fiona returned in six months, she'd be a valuable asset to the unit. Jane sighed and said she'd look at her schedules.

It took her nearly an hour to sort out, but she could release Fiona and not have to rely too much on agency nurses. It meant moving a lot of people around, altering rosters that she'd already posted. But it seemed to be possible. Just.

'It's taken me a lot of trouble to work out a plan,' she told Fiona when she came back for her answer, 'but I think I've done it. You can go on your course.'

'Thanks, Jane. That's good of you. And I'm sure you'll never miss me when I'm away.'

Only then did Jane suspect a tiny touch of spite, and wondered if in some way she had been tricked. But she thought not. It was just paranoia, after being attacked.

*   *   *

She was still in her office when Chris came in later that day. As he usually did when no one was looking, he kissed her. Then he ran his hand down her back. 'Still taking it easy?'

'It's impossible to do any work here. My nurses just won't let me.'

'They'd have me to answer to if they did. Now, still determined to grab what you can from life?'

'Yes. Do I gather that you've got something in mind?'

'Just a chance, a possibility,' he said casually. Then he looked a little doubtful. 'I've been looking at the work rosters. We've both got two days off towards the end of next week.'

'True. And before you ask me, by that time I intend to be fully better.'

'Well, partly better,' he said. He seemed to be having difficulty in deciding what to say next. He kissed her on the neck but it was in an almost abstracted way.

'Come on,' she said. 'You'll feel better when you've told me.'

'Yes.' He took a deep breath. 'This is something I've never quite asked anyone before. It started some weeks ago. You know how I rely on Mrs Mansell? My life would be impossible without her. Well, she said some time ago that she'd like to go and stay with her daughter. So I decided to take these two days off to stay with James while she went visiting. I wondered if… James asked if you could come. I wondered if you'd like to come and stay in a hotel near us? Just for a couple of nights? We're going to stay near Whitby.'

'I'd love to come,' she said doubtfully. 'But in a hotel near you? Couldn't I stay in your hotel?'

'Well, this was all arranged a while ago. Before you…before I really knew you. It was James's idea, he was really keen. We're going camping.'

'Camping?'

'I'm afraid so. Like I said, it's not my idea.'

'In a little tent with a campfire?'

He looked horrified. 'No. Not yet. In a few years perhaps, when he's older. But this place is quite civilised. There's a big tent with bedrooms, a kitchen and an awning to eat under. There's a table and chairs, a stove and a fridge and a barbecue and the hot showers are very close. But it is under canvas and James is very excited.'

'How many bedrooms?'

'Three.'

'Then I'll have one. I'm coming camping with you, Chris. Did you know that you were talking to an ex-Queen's Guide? In my youth I spent more time under canvas than I did in a bedroom.'

'But you're not…you're not well yet.'

'I'm well enough. And someone has to look after the greenhorns.' Then a thought struck her and she looked at him anxiously. 'You do want me, don't you? It won't be awkward—me and you and James?'

'We'll make allowances,' he said.

Erica phoned Jane the next day. 'I'm coming back to the nurses' home to get a few more things,' she said. 'I know it's silly but I don't want to go in there on my own. Will you be there tonight?'

'Of course I will if you want me to. Just tell me roughly the time you think you'll arrive.'

'About seven. I'll borrow Matt's car. And we can have a cup of tea and a chat.'

Jane could tell that Erica was nervous when she stood where Martin had confronted her, when for a moment she had been in fear of her life. But then she walked into her room, looked at her pictures and the little things that had made it her home, and she smiled. 'I'm all right now,' she said. 'I could move straight back in if I wanted. I was happy here, it was a haven for me.'

'Was?' asked Jane. 'Have you decided to move out?'

'Matt's invited me to stay with him as long as I like. I can have my own bedroom, he says we can live and share like two friends if that's what I want. Did you know that he shared a flat with two girls when he was training? And all perfectly proper.'

'Do you want to be friends and be perfectly proper?'

'No,' Erica said after a while. 'I know people will say that I'm taking up with Matt because I'm on the rebound and that I ought to wait a while. But you've got to take a risk sometimes, Jane. Otherwise you might miss something really good.' She looked at her friend and added, 'And you're taking a chance, too, aren't you?'

'Yes, I suppose I am.'

'And you're happy about it aren't you?'

She had to pause but then she said, 'Yes, very happy.'

'Good. I like Chris, I think he's wonderful. Now I've got all I want from here, let's go to your room and have a cup of tea.'

Jane had been turning out her drawers, looking for

clothes suitable for a camping weekend. And she'd found something that was most unsuitable. 'What's this?' Erica asked, looking at the dress on the bed. 'It's lovely.'

Jane picked it up, a dark blue silk dress that she had bought three years before, worn once and had never had the chance to wear again. She held it against herself, stroked the fabric.

Erica noticed her silence. 'Bring back memories?' she asked gently.

'I wore it when I went to a party with my husband. It was the last time we went out together. Three years ago. I've never worn it since.'

'Then find a chance to wear it or send it to a charity shop, otherwise it's just cluttering up your wardrobe and your life.'

The words sounded brutal, but Jane knew they hadn't been meant that way. 'I'm going to wear it,' she said after a while. 'I look good in it.'

'Good. And make sure you wear it soon.'

The next five days seemed to pass all too slowly. Jane dug out garments she hadn't worn in years, but had intended to wear when she'd come north. And she was enjoying herself. All they would need to be happy was good weather.

Two days before they were to go, Chris dropped in her room and said, 'I've been checking. There's a very good children's club on this site. I've arranged for James to go to it on the second evening just for a couple of hours. So if you like to pack just one nice dress we could have a civilised dinner in a nearby hotel.'

'We're going to be civilised every night,' she told him. But she thought of the blue silk dress and decided to take it.

Then it was the day they were to travel. She got to her desk early that morning, worked steadily through her paperwork. There would be no worries about work left undone. Then at five she scampered home, had a swift shower and changed. Her bag was already packed.

She was going on holiday with Chris and with James. They were going away, not as lovers but as a family. And she was a full part. She had told him he could bring some wine but she would organise the food. And she'd done so.

This would be a new step forward in the relationship and she felt just a little on edge. She knew that when they came back, things would have changed. They would know each other much better. She hoped that would be a good thing.

Chris arrived in his car five minutes later, a grinning, waving James in the back seat. She was waiting outside for him, dressed in serviceable jeans and a dark shirt, a box of food by her feet, her weekend bag in her hand.

A couple of her friends came out of the nurses' home, smiled at her and looked thoughtfully at Chris's car. She didn't care who saw her or guessed what she was doing. This was part of the new Jane. She would seize what she could.

He kissed her on the cheek and they drove off into the warm evening.

'We're going camping,' yelled James. 'We're going to sleep in a tent and have a campfire. I've brought your blanket and Daddy's bought us all real feather headdresses and we can all be Indians. Fantastic! D'you want to put your headdress on now, Jane?'

So she did. Who cared who might see her? She was happy.

They were out of town now, driving along the coast road, with glimpses of the sea and the greenery of the Wolds. After a while James became absorbed in watching the countryside and Chris murmured, 'We should be in luck with the weather—the forecast is warm and dry for the next few days. You know, I've thought about the first time I'd take you away for the weekend. I thought it would be just the two of us, somewhere like London or Paris or a fine country hotel. Not camping, with my son in tow.'

'I'm happy with things as they are,' she said. 'As far as I'm concerned, you and James come as a package.'

'What about sleeping arrangements?'

'One thing is certain, we're not going to embarrass him. I sleep in my own bedroom.'

'Of course. But he is a heavy sleeper. And whatever we do we can do quietly. It can still be fun, though.'

He glanced at her and the promise in his eyes made her blush. Her entire body grew warm at the idea. 'I'm sure it can,' she said primly.

He reached over and squeezed her hand. 'Just being with you will be plenty,' he said.

It didn't take them long to get to the site and Jane approved of it at once. It was clean, with a good little shop and café. Their tent was far superior to the military green canvas ones she used to camp in. A warden showed them round, explained where everything was.

'There's a campfire!' James said, pointing to their barbecue pit. 'A real campfire. Not like our little barbecue.'

'Sort of a campfire,' said Jane. To Chris she said, 'Why don't you take James for a walk round and I'll start the evening meal?'

'But I thought the first night we could have something in the café and—'

'This is my province and, believe me, I'm good at it.'

'There are sides to you I didn't know about,' he muttered, but he did as she said.

She had planned it all. First she started the barbecue, then set the table and put out rolls and salad. It was still very warm so they could sit outside quite happily. When the barbecue was ready she put on the sausages and kebabs she had brought. Dinner would be served as soon as the two returned.

James was really excited by the barbecue—the campfire—and had to sit by it to eat in his headdress and blanket. He loved helping to cook. But soon he was tired, and Chris took him to shower and then put him into bed while Jane washed up.

It was getting dark. She poured herself another glass of wine and sat to wait for him. Eventually he joined her.

'I've never seen a child go to sleep so quickly,' he said. 'And now I feel guilty. You seem to be doing everything, this isn't a holiday for you. Most women would think this is a duty, not a pleasure.'

'I love it,' she said. 'I feel I'm part of a family and that hasn't happened to me in ages.'

He put his arm round her, kissed her. 'That's a very nice thing to say.'

'It's a very nice thing to feel.' Then, unable to help it, she yawned.

He laughed. 'Is that a hint?'

'No. It's just been a good, long, exciting day.'

'And is the day now over?'

She looked at the tent behind them, with two bedrooms on one side of the central living section, another bedroom on the other side. Hers was the other bedroom. 'I'm going to shower and clean my teeth,' she said. 'Then I'll go to bed. Why don't you make sure that James is asleep then come and give me a good-night kiss?'

'All right.'

'And, whatever you do, we've got to be quiet.' She went to fetch her towel.

Once in her bedroom she sat on her campbed. It squeaked. She thought for a moment then pulled the mattress onto the ground and made the bed there. She had never had a mattress when she'd been a Guide.

Her light was out but there was a dim glow through the canvas from the camp lights outside. She unzipped her door as it was still a warm night. Then she pulled her nightie over her head, lay there naked for him. It was a gesture of giving.

There was a rustle at the door, she could see the outline of him against the dim light. In the softest of whispers she called, 'I'm here, on the floor.'

He knelt by her side, felt for her. His hands touched her hair, her shoulders, her body. She reached for him.

He took her hands, gently lifted them so that they

were behind her head. Then he crouched over her, kissed her.

She whispered, 'We must be quiet. Don't try to say anything, just be with me.' Then she found that he, too, was naked. It was odd, it was exciting.

They made love with the passion she remembered but always trying to be silent. Even their heavy breathing was held in check. But when they exploded together in a joint but noiseless climax, she felt that the intensity had almost increased.

He lay with her there for a while. Then she told him that they had to do it again that way some time, but now she was going to sleep and he must go to his own bed.

'I wish I'd been a Scout,' he muttered. She had to bury her face in her pillow to stop herself giggling.

It was fine again next day. They had bacon sandwiches, which tasted even better because they were eaten in the open air. Then they drove into Whitby. All three of them were dressed in T-shirt and shorts. Chris made them all smear on sunblock, and gave James a baseball cap to wear. Good.

She liked Whitby, the steep-sided little town with the river as centre. They walked to the end of the pier, James in the middle, holding a hand each. She turned to look at the abbey on the top of the cliffs, the houses clinging to the hillside, and smiled.

'What are you thinking?' he asked. 'You look happy.'

She answered without considering what her answer might mean, what he might make of it. 'I was just thinking that we seem to be a family,' she said. 'And we're...' She didn't know how to go on.

'And we're taking it easy, deciding on nothing, just seeing how we get on,' he said. 'That's fine.'

'Can we play on the sand now, Daddy?' James asked.

That evening she went out just with Chris. James went to an organised party with other children. Both she and Chris talked to the organisers and felt confident that James would be happy. They had Chris's mobile number and he never would be more than fifteen minutes away.

She changed into the blue silk dress. He wore light chinos and a white shirt. They had been told that a pub nearby served excellent meals so they sat outside on the terrace and ate overlooking the sea. She couldn't remember being so happy.

'This is so good,' she said. 'I am enjoying myself.'

'You really are?' His voice was questioning, doubtful.

She took his arm, pulled him round to face her. 'Chris, I am enjoying myself and I'm doing so because I'm here with you. Why should you doubt me?'

He put his arms round her shoulders, she could feel the warmth of his flesh against hers. 'I could never doubt you, sweetheart. But sometimes I do worry about you.'

'Worry about me? Chris, why? Isn't everything fine between us?' Now she was feeling worried.

'Everything is fine. But just for a moment then you looked sad. Then you looked down at your hand and twisted your wedding ring. I've seen you do that before. You were thinking about your husband, weren't you?'

She thought about that and said, 'Chris, I'm here

with you. And I can tell you that I haven't enjoyed myself so much, been so happy, in years. It was just a passing thought.'

He took her hand in his. 'Your husband died. You loved him very much, I can tell. Now you are here, a young woman in the prime of life. Whenever you catch yourself enjoying yourself, do you wish he were here with you, sharing your pleasure?'

For a while she was silent. Then she said, 'You want an honest answer don't you? I'll try, Chris, but it will be hard because often I don't know what I'm feeling myself. Feelings sort of creep up on me when I'm not expecting them.'

She looked at the sun turning the sea gold, heard the chatter of the other guests.

'When he first died—no, months before that, while he was alive but only just, whenever something nice happened to me—I wanted to share it with him. And it was impossible. Now I'm getting my life together I tend just to think of myself. And I think of you, and of me and you. I think of us a lot. But I have to admit that every now and then I wonder what life would be like if…if he were still with me.'

She looked at him, saw his absorbed face, felt the tightness of his hand round hers. 'But I am so happy here with you, Chris! It's just…just different. You do see that, don't you?'

'Of course I do!' Suddenly, he pulled her to him, kissed her hard on the lips. 'Jane, you've heard me talk, I've never used a four-letter word to you, have I?'

'Certainly not,' she said primly, adding, 'Why would you want to anyway?'

'Love. L-O-V-E. It's a four-letter word. I've never said I loved you.'

Now they were getting serious. She wondered what he was going to say next. 'I've never said I love you either,' she said. 'It's all a bit…final.'

'Final. That's a good word. It's an ending word.' He went on, obviously choosing his words with care, 'I've thought of love quite a lot. Too many people say it too easily, it doesn't mean very much. But I want it to mean something to me, and I suspect it means something to you, too.'

'Go on,' she said.

'I think we are moving towards a relationship that means love. I've thought it before and I've been wrong, so this time I'm determined to get it right. And you, you feel the same way?'

'We're a cautious pair, aren't we?' she asked. 'But, yes, you're right. I don't want to hurry, but I feel we're moving towards something. And it'll be worth waiting for, I'm sure.'

She looked around her and suddenly her voice was joyous. 'There is another four-letter word,' she said. 'It only needs one letter changed. What about live? L-I-V-E? For a while let's just live. We've a good idea of the happiness the future will bring. Love is growing between us. We'll wait till it's certain, and then we'll both know what to do.'

'Of course we will,' he said.

CHAPTER NINE

THEY went back to collect an exhausted but happy James. He wanted to sit by his campfire for a while and Jane lit it for him. But soon he fell asleep while sitting on Jane's lap and she carried him to bed.

That night Chris came to her bed on the ground again and again they were silent.

'This is getting to be a habit,' he whispered.

'One I could get to like,' she whispered back.

Next morning they started another good day. They decided that they'd come back to the campsite some time in the future, perhaps for longer. Then they went for a drive and a walk on the moors behind Whitby.

It was agreed that they'd get back to Chris's house quite early. In spite of having slept so well, James was still tired, it would be best to put him to bed promptly.

'You will stay the night?' he asked.

'If I'm invited,' she said.

As ever, unpacking after a holiday wasn't half as much fun as packing for one. Jane went into the kitchen to make sandwiches while Chris saw to James and then checked his mail and his phone messages. He seemed to be quite a long time, and when he returned Jane could see by his disturbed face that something was wrong.

'James is watching a video,' he said. 'He won't bother us for a while. And we need to talk.'

174

Now Jane was disturbed herself. She had never seen him so ill at ease. 'What's wrong?'

'There was a message on my answering machine that I was to phone my wife at once. I just have done.'

'You said she was out of your life for good, that she would never be a problem! The divorce was going through. And now she's phoning you. I think I'd better go, Chris.'

'No, wait. Just listen. This concerns you as well as me.'

'She's talking about me? How could she? What does she know about me?'

He sighed. 'Please, Jane, sit down. Listen to me and then make your mind up. I'm as upset by this as you are.'

Jane hadn't realised that she'd sprung to her feet. But now she sat, eyed him warily. 'I'm listening,' she said. 'But when you said that she was your wife it made me realise that...that we've been committing adultery.'

He sighed again, rubbed his hand through his hair. 'It doesn't feel like that to me. Or to you. But just listen.'

'Eleanor—my wife—still has some regard for me. And for James. She'd received a call from her sister saying that I'd fallen for some terrible woman who would ruin my life and also James's and it was up to Eleanor to do something about it.'

Jane stared at Chris unbelievingly. 'Her sister? You mean Fiona?'

'I mean Fiona.'

Jane remembered that sly look Fiona had given her

when last they'd parted. 'I didn't realise she hated us enough to do that,' she said.

'Well, apparently she did. But Eleanor knows her sister, they never really got on. She didn't believe the story but felt that she ought to phone me to check.'

'So what did you say?'

'I told her that I'd met a woman, that we had a lot in common, that we were both a bit cautious but I had great hopes that something would come of things.'

'And she said?'

'She wished me luck. She said she'd hurry up the divorce, she might get married again herself. She also said that if I was really serious then I could tell you why we split up. Do you want to know?'

'You know I do!' Jane couldn't help saying. 'But first of all, what does she look like?'

Now he smiled. 'The very opposite of you. She seldom smiled. Dark hair, very dark complexion. A bit taller than you but thinner. Not a great deal of—'

'I can guess,' Jane said. 'What about her character?'

'She was—is—an archaeologist. Says that she doesn't like most people she meets and can't be bothered to hide the fact. She's clever but remote.'

'So why did you part?'

'I think a better question would be why did we get married? But we did and we seemed happy enough, each going our separate ways. But then she fell pregnant—an accident really, she admitted, her fault. I was delighted. She wasn't really looking forward to having the child but everyone told her that the minute she saw it she'd change. You've been a midwife, you know what I mean.'

'I know. Some people say it's just hormones, just

oxytocin that does it. But I don't agree, I think it's magic. They way a mother looks at her child for the first time, that's magic.'

Chris looked sad. 'True, I've seen it myself, it is magic. It just didn't work for Eleanor. She could never bond with James.'

Jane stared at him disbelievingly. 'What?'

'She never felt any emotion for her child at all. She didn't dislike him, she wasn't ever cruel, she just wasn't interested. She had counselling, hormone treatment, everything possible. But it never worked. And because of that I loved James more than ever. Eventually she told me that she knew she never would love the child so she would leave him and me together. It would be better if we parted. And after a while I agreed.'

Jane was both amazed and appalled, she'd never heard a story like this. 'Did she love you?'

'In her cool way, I think so.'

'And did you love her?'

'I learned…slowly…not to.'

'And did it hurt?'

'Oh, it hurt. Sometimes it still does.'

'And are you afraid of it happening again? With me?'

'I was afraid of something happening again. But then I met you and I'm willing to take a risk. That is, if you will.'

She stood, walked over and kissed him. 'I think I'd better go home tonight,' she said. 'I still feel the same about you but I have thinking to do. And I'd like it if you were properly divorced.'

'I'll see to it. But I do believe we could make each other very happy.'

He kissed her. Then she left.

As she took a taxi home she felt bewildered. How did this story affect her and him? She found she could even feel sorry for Eleanor. She could understand his caution, too. But then she decided they could work it out. She had left in too much of a hurry. When she got back she would phone and say so.

There was a message on her own answering machine when she reached her little room. Dr Lansing wanted her to call him urgently and had left a mobile number. Dr Lansing? Then she remembered, the young doctor who had treated her in A and E. Feeling rather apprehensive, she phoned him at once.

'In fact, I'm working in A and E at the moment,' he said. 'Would you come over and have a word?'

'What about?'

'I really rather would speak to you in person.'

'All right. I'll be there in ten minutes.' Too much excitement today, she thought to herself.

Fortunately A and E wasn't too busy. Dr Lansing took her for a cup of tea and asked her in general how she was.

'I'm fine, Doctor, but a bit mystified. What's the problem?'

'Something came up in your blood tests, I just wanted to satisfy myself and you.' He handed her a small parcel. 'Here's the kit, you're a nurse, you know how to take the test. Go in that cubicle there.'

She looked at the parcel, looked at him but said nothing. Then she went to the cubicle he had pointed to. What seemed like an age later, she came out. 'Positive,' she said.

'So you're pregnant. Er...I hope it's good news.'

Jane checked her watch. It was only nine o'clock. She phoned Chris. 'I need to come round. Is James in bed?'

'He's in bed. Jane, you sound odd. Are you in trouble?'

'I'll be there in fifteen minutes. I won't be staying.'

As she drove to his house she thought of the positive assurance she had given him that there would be no consequences if they made love. Then she thought over how she had taken the pill that should have stopped any consequences and worked out where she had gone wrong. She had forgotten to take them for a few days after they'd had sex the first time! Well, that was her fault.

As she drove into his drive she realised she was still wearing the clothes she had worn for the holiday. No time to change. When she got into the house she noticed that Chris had had time to shower and change. He was wearing a shirt and jeans. She thought she'd never seen him looking so attractive. Or, now, so unavailable.

When he bent to kiss her she turned her head so that he kissed her only on the cheek. 'I've heard and said this so many times,' she said. 'We have to talk.'

'You're sure you don't want time to think first? Jane, this is upsetting, I know, but we can work things out and—'

'It's not about you, it's about me. Something I would have told you in time.'

He took her into his study, asked her if she wanted a drink. Yes, she did, but she wouldn't have one now.

'We seem to be going over old relationships this evening,' she said. 'Now it's my turn. Remember I told you about my husband—well, I missed a bit of the story out. Just before John got ill I...I got pregnant. It was something we both wanted, had planned for. We were both delighted—especially him. Then after two months I miscarried. You know, one in four pregnancies fail.'

'I know,' he said. 'It's very upsetting but there's usually no long-term ill effects. You can try again.'

'He was ill, we couldn't try again. And I became used to the idea of never having a child of my own.'

'I'm sorry. Jane, you should have told me, I would have understood.'

'It's all in the past. Now I want you just to sit there, listen and not say anything. Don't say anything!' She realised that her voice was now almost hysterical and saw the alarm on his face.

'Of course I won't.'

'Right, then, I'm pregnant.'

She watched his face closely, tried to read the emotions playing across it. Shock, bewilderment—even a touch of pleasure? She couldn't tell.

'I don't understand... You told me...'

'It appears the women in your life aren't lucky. Two of them getting pregnant without really wanting to.'

'But, Jane, I... You know I'll... We have to plan and...'

'I asked you not to say anything. This is all too much for me. I was beginning to think I could have a relationship with you, in spite of my earlier fears. I thought there might be something there eventually but I didn't want to start like this. I've got to think about things. Got to consider what I'm going to do.'

He tensed. 'You're not going to…'

'No, of course I'm not. But for a while I need to think. I wasn't going to tell you, but I felt you're entitled to know. Now, please, Chris, leave me alone for a while. I'll tell you how I think in a week or so.'

'But there's more than you in this! I'm involved, too!'

'You're as involved as I want you to be! All I want is some time. I could cope with thinking about you and me and James. But you and me and James and a baby is a lot more.'

He was a silent for a while. 'A week to think,' he said. 'All right. But, Jane, then we talk.'

She nodded. Then she left.

It was lonely in the nurses' home without Erica to confide in. If ever she had needed someone to talk to, it was now. But Erica was gone. Jane lay in bed, her thoughts whirling. Just what should she do? She could tell that in spite of his shock, Chris had been rather pleased with the thought of a baby. But how did she feel? Somehow, the emotional strain of taking on all of them seemed too much. She was going to get hurt again, she knew she was. Perhaps she should cut her losses. Leave here, have her baby, never, ever put her trust in love again. She had made herself even more vulnerable and she hated it.

Next morning she went back to work. She spent half an hour splashing cold water onto her red-rimmed eyes and eventually, with the aid of some heavy make-up, she looked reasonable. She'd have to meet him. She'd have to work with him. So she was going to be tough about it. All she had left now was her pride.

In the afternoon there was a minor crisis. Baby Pendleton had been born at thirty-two weeks, was now at thirty-four weeks and had been doing reasonably well. But suddenly there was cause for alarm. The baby's temperature was up, she was in distress and Jane wasn't very happy with her shallow breathing. A doctor had to be summoned. Chris was on call. Jane asked a nurse to bleep him.

It was her duty to be at Chris's side while he looked at the observations, examined the little mite. She did her job professionally, answering his questions, but always avoiding his eye. This was her job. Finally he made his assessment, told her that he didn't think there was too much to worry about but that he should be informed at once if there was any further change in the baby's state.

'I'll see to that Mr Fielding.'

'Good. Now, Jane, d'you think there's any chance of a coffee in your room?'

'Please, sit in my room if you wish. I'll see that a nurse brings you a coffee but I'm needed here on the ward.'

'You're not needed on the ward as much as I need to talk to you. I've been thinking and—'

'A week, I said. We'll talk then.'

He looked at her hopelessly, then walked out of the ward.

Jane wondered how she'd get through the next few days, but in the end the problem solved itself.

Sometimes it just happened that way. The flow of pre-term babies suddenly increased—in fact, it doubled. Most of them weren't seriously ill, they just required patient and time-consuming care until they were strong enough to be sent home. There were observations, feeding, changing and cleaning, and the ever-anxious parents to calm and explain things to.

Jane and her staff were madly busy. Fortunately they were now a team. There was always a readiness to alter a shift, to stay a little longer, to work non-stop without a break. The babies came first. And Jane was pleased about this. She felt she had accomplished something.

Of course, she had to see Chris. He, too, was over-worked. But a couple of times he did find time to ask her if they could have a quiet word. Each time she said no. She was too busy and there was nothing to say. And after that he seemed to keep out of her way, their contact was purely professional. She told herself it was what she wanted. But it hurt.

There was just one odd incident. Matt had been working on the unit all morning and she had invited him to her office to grab a coffee and a chocolate bis-cuit.

'Jane? Can I risk irritating you?' He looked sheep-ish. 'Just for one minute and then I'll shut up.'

'I'm irritable enough already, but go on.'

'I owe you a lot. You brought me and Erica together and that's...well, it's been good. I just want you to know that Chris is basically a good man, that he...he thinks a lot of you. And this week, working for him has been sheer hell. Can't you get together again and give us all an easier life?'

She had to laugh, though she wanted to cry. 'I'd like to help, Matt, but even for you I can't. Now, another chocolate biscuit?'

It happened that evening. She had come in from work, would get something to eat later. Now she was sitting in her room, looking through her photograph album. Pictures of herself and John. It was something she often did. But tonight it was different.

The pictures were still there—but they were only pictures, little squares of card. The memories were there, too. But that's all they were. They were things from the past. She gazed at a picture of herself, happy, smiling. And younger. She was no longer that unsophisticated girl. Her life had been tragic—but she had come through it. She was older, wiser.

It struck her that she couldn't spend her life mourning the past. And then it struck her that she now had to start thinking about what would be the best for two, not one. She was having a baby.

She reached out for her phone.

'Chris? It's Jane.'

'Jane? Everything OK?' His voice was cautious, he wasn't sure what she wanted. She felt guilty at the pain she knew she'd put him through.

'Everything is fine, really fine. I just want an answer to a question. How d'you feel about having a brother or a sister for James?'

'I've thought about it a lot. And I can't think of anything more marvellous. So long as he or she comes in a package with a mother.'

'And I can't think of anything I want more for my

baby than you as a father and James as a brother. Can you get away this evening?'

She thought she had never heard such joy in a voice. 'Mrs Mansell will happily babysit. Shall I come round?'

'No. Meet me at the car park on the south side. In half an hour?'

'I'll be there. And Jane, I—'

'When we meet,' she said.

It was hot. It had been a hot summer but this evening was very hot. Jane arrived at the south side car park early and found some shade to sit in. She needed to be calm and collected when Chris arrived.

She saw the big burgundy car drive up and he jumped out. He was dressed, like her, in shorts and T-shirt. She walked over to meet him.

She didn't quite know what to say to him, which was fine. He obviously wasn't sure what to say to her. 'People stay close to what they know,' he said. 'If we walk along the beach we'll soon be on our own.'

'Good. I'd like that.' So they set off across the hot sand, the cliffs to their right, the sea to their left. After a while she took off her sandals and walked to the water's edge, splashing in it. He did the same. Then he held her hand and they walked onwards.

Behind them the sounds of holidaymaking slowly died away and all they could hear was the beat of the waves and the piercing cry of the gulls.

'I came down here the first time I arrived in Denham,' she said. 'I was here before I went for the interview. And met you for the first time. So coming here is like a beginning and an end.'

'Or a new beginning,' he said.

He led her out of the water and across the sand to the foot of the cliff. There they found a rock to perch on and again stared out to sea in silence for a while.

'I don't know where to start,' he said. 'There's so much to say to you that I don't know where to start.'

'I do.' She spread her left hand, looked at her wedding ring. Then she took it off and kissed it—and this time put it into her pocket. 'This is the ending,' she said. 'I'm not going to wear it, but I'm going to keep it. You don't mind?'

'Not at all. It has memories and they're part of you. I want you to keep it. To remind you of John.'

'He would have liked you. But now he's gone and we're still here. I've just learned. Life must move on.'

He edged closer to her and put his arm round her shoulders. She leaned against him, felt his warmth against hers. 'True.' He took her hand, rubbed a finger against the little band of white where her wedding ring had been. 'You took off your ring. A part of your life ending, another part beginning. Remember at the camp last week? When you said you were going to live?'

'I remember. And I meant it. Finding out that I…that we…well, it was such a shock. I didn't know what to do. But now I quite like the idea of having a baby.' She looked at him anxiously. 'Chris, you're not just saying that you're happy because you feel you've got to?'

'Certainly not! For a long time James was the centre of my life. But now you and James and little baby Fielding, I'll love you all.'

'Baby Fielding?'

'Well, you'll have to marry me now. Make an honest man of me. And a happy one.'

'You're sure that... You think that we can...?'

'I've never been more certain of anything,' he said.

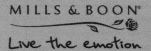

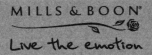

Medical Romance™

SURGEON IN CRISIS by Jennifer Taylor

A posting to Mexico with Worlds Together was going to be an adventure for Sister Rachel Hart. And when she met the medical aid organisation's founder and surgeon, Shiloh Smith, her heart really started to pound. But Shiloh was a widower, and didn't believe that special love came more than once for anyone...

THE POLICE SURGEON'S RESCUE
by Abigail Gordon

Working for GP and police surgeon Dr Blake Pemberton is as close a brush with the law as Nurse Helena Harris wants. But then she finds herself testifying against a gang who threatened her father's life. Blake is determined to protect Helena, and she soon finds herself falling for this very courageous doctor...

THE HEART CONSULTANT'S LOVER
by Kate Hardy

Miranda Turner gave up on love a long time ago. Now she's wedded to her career – and her prestigious new job as consultant in cardiology. Senior Registrar Jack Sawyer is furious at Miranda's appointment. He wants to hate her, but can't help respecting her. And soon their powerful attraction explodes into a steamy affair!

On sale 2nd April 2004

Available at most branches of WHSmith, Tesco, Martins, Borders, Eason, Sainsbury's and all good paperback bookshops.

0304/03b

FREE
4 BOOKS
AND A SURPRISE GIFT!

We would like to take this opportunity to thank you for reading this Mills & Boon® book by offering you the chance to take FOUR more specially selected titles from the Medical Romance™ series absolutely FREE! We're also making this offer to introduce you to the benefits of the Reader Service™ —

★ FREE home delivery
★ FREE monthly Newsletter
★ FREE gifts and competitions
★ Exclusive Reader Service discount
★ Books available before they're in the shops

Accepting these FREE books and gift places you under no obligation to buy; you may cancel at any time, even after receiving your free shipment. Simply complete your details below and return the entire page to the address below. *You don't even need a stamp!*

YES! Please send me 4 free Medical Romance books and a surprise gift. I understand that unless you hear from me, I will receive 6 superb new titles every month for just £2.69 each, postage and packing free. I am under no obligation to purchase any books and may cancel my subscription at any time. The free books and gift will be mine to keep in any case.

M4ZEF

Ms/Mrs/Miss/Mr ....Initials ....
BLOCK CAPITALS PLEASE

Surname ....

Address ....

....

....Postcode ....

Send this whole page to:
UK: FREEPOST CN81, Croydon, CR9 3WZ
EIRE: PO Box 4546, Kilcock, County Kildare (stamp required)

Offer valid in UK and Eire only and not available to current Reader Service subscribers to this series. We reserve the right to refuse an application and applicants must be aged 18 years or over. Only one application per household. Terms and prices subject to change without notice. Offer expires 30th June 2004. As a result of this application, you may receive offers from Harlequin Mills & Boon and other carefully selected companies. If you would prefer not to share in this opportunity please write to The Data Manager at the address above.

Mills & Boon® is a registered trademark owned by Harlequin Mills & Boon Limited.
Medical Romance™ is being used as a trademark.
The Reader Service™ is being used as a trademark.